Tempest of Secrets

Sofia Costa Book 7

By Georgia Wagner

© 2025 Georgia Wagner. All rights reserved.

This is a work of fiction; names, characters, places, and incidents are products of the author's imagination or used fictitiously—any resemblance to actual persons, living or dead, or actual events is purely coincidental.

No part of this book may be reproduced, distributed, or transmitted in any form or by any means, electronic or mechanical, including photocopying, recording, or by any information storage and retrieval system, without the prior written permission of the publisher, except in the case of brief quotations embodied in reviews.

For permissions, contact GeorgiaWagner.com. "Georgia Wagner" and the names of characters and distinctive likenesses are trademarks or registered trademarks of the author. If this is an eBook, it is licensed to the original purchaser for personal use only and may not be resold or shared.

CHAPTER 1

Sofia Costa watched the storm roll in and held her breath.

The charcoal clouds mirrored the storm-gray of her own eyes—sharp, observant eyes that missed nothing as they tracked the advancing wall of rain across the horizon. She brushed a strand of dark, wavy hair from her face, tucking it back into the messy bun secured with her ever-present 2b pencil. The scar along her left eyebrow tingled as it always did before bad weather, a personal barometer she'd come to rely on.

Sofia adjusted the collar of her practical jacket, layering it closer against the rising wind. Her olive skin had darkened slightly during her time in Hawaii, though she'd spent most of it indoors pursuing leads rather than lounging on beaches. The yellow pencil suddenly threatened to blow out of her hair, and she secured it in the belt loop of her jeans.

They'd threatened to take Julian's sister, and so the two of them had flown halfway around the world to where Mila Varga worked at a marine biology outpost on a small island near Japan.

They were going to meet Mila. Sofia wasn't sure how she felt about this—she'd already met Julian's brother, and that had nearly ended in a double homicide.

As Sofia and Julian disembarked, she glanced back at the old vessel that had carried them from the larger island.

The ferry bell tolled once, a dull iron note swallowed by wind. Water slapped the hull in short, angry strokes, the color of wet slate; even the foam looked gray beneath a sky cinched tight with cloud. Gulls wheeled low, as if some invisible hand held them by a string and tugged them toward land. Lines creaked. Ropes hummed. The island rose like the back of a sleeping animal, all dark ridges and lacquered jungle, the palm crowns stiff against the sharpening gusts.

On the quay, dockworkers paused in their movements as the gangplank thudded down. A collective hitch in breath. Eyes slid over them—past them—as though the wind were blowing the foreigners sideways out of focus. Sofia heard the word for storm spoken in two tongues, the rounder vowels of Uchinaaguchi tucked beneath the flatter consonants of standard Japanese. Taifū, she filed away, and kusho—an old fisherman's mutter, prayer folded into practical weather. One younger man murmured, "Muri da yo," under his breath as he shouldered a crate. He wasn't looking at the sea.

Julian didn't seem to feel the wind. He moved through it, away from their ferry, along the cobbled island streets. No lopsided grin today, no courteous banter with the deckhands lining the wharf. His blue eyes were narrow, scanning the pier, the parked kei trucks, the strip of shops with their salt-fogged windows and faded ice cream posters.

He handed her his phone without looking at her. A single message glowed on the cracked screen.

Staying up at the ridge guesthouse. *Promise I'll lay low. No lights. No calls. Just till this blows over. I'm safe. Love you.*

Time stamp: last night, 23:42.

"She always promised," he said, voice low, as they fell in step along the pier. "When we were kids, she'd swear on anything. Our mother's favorite record, the stupid cherry tree in the garden." The corner of his mouth tightened. "She'd climb anyway."

Sofia watched his pace lengthen, purpose telescoping his stride. He didn't look at the map she'd sketched in pencil on the ferry. He moved as if he'd known this path all his life. "Why here?" she asked, not to slow him, but to hear it from him.

"Whales," he said. "The foundation's marine grants kept a roof on that guesthouse. She started advising them a year ago—seasonal research, coral rehab, getting kids in the water." He blew out a breath that wasn't a laugh. "It made Josef furious. Image is currency, and she was spending the family name without his permission. But she could thread both worlds when it mattered. Tea with donors in Tokyo, then barefoot on a boat with students the next morning. She wasn't pretending to be two people," he added, more to himself than to Sofia. "She just... refused to amputate parts of herself to make him comfortable."

"You don't blame her for that," Sofia said.

"For refusing to be less?" He shook his head once. "I wish I'd been better at it."

A memory of the taunting voice skimmed the surface of the wind—*We're going to take her*—and Sofia felt the old, clean heat rise in her chest. Nuno had tried to trace the call while she watched city lights run out along the Barcelona ring road. But no luck, the voice had used a burner.

The climb cut steeply away from the

harbor, stone stairs slick with salt and beginning rain. Hibiscus leaves slapped their calves. Geckos chirped like tiny metronomes from the concrete walls. As they rose, the wind grew knifed with sand and the sound of the sea changed shape—less splash, more roar, a giant drawing breath somewhere they couldn't see.

The guesthouse sat where the ridge softened and the jungle thinned, a lovely old wooden structure that had been kissed too hard and too long by salt. Window shutters hung cocked, their paint eaten to the grain. A wetsuit—small, black, patched at the knee—swayed from a rusted line.

Julian shouldered the sliding door; it stuttered, then gave. Inside, the air smelled of iodine and wet books. Posters of fish species peeled from the walls in elegant curls. A tide chart was pinned above a desk, a chair pushed all the way under a table and squared to the planks; coffee grounds scattered on the counter like black confetti, fresh and damp; no mug anywhere. A kettle still warm under her palm. A pair of deck shoes aligned heel-to-heel at the mat. The floor carried fine tracks of sand not yet settled into the grain—two sets, crossed, one lighter, one heavier, both recent.

Julian took the first door; it rattled against the stopper with a bang that made the geckos fall briefly silent. "Mila!" He was riffling drawers, unstacking books, the careful hands she knew from safecracker work turned suddenly clumsy. Fear had a way of loosening even the most precise grip. "Mila—answer me!"

In the bedroom, the bedspread was hand-dyed indigo, the pattern of waves repeating in neat chiasms.

Julian was in the bathroom now, the mirrored cabinet yawning open, bottles splayed on the counter. "Her toothbrush is dry," he said, voice frayed. "She was here earlier. Her bag—" He yanked the closet door. An empty shelf gaped back.

"Goddammit." The word escaped Julian as he threw open every cabinet, then spun to face the hall, his fists white knots at his sides. All the control in him, the play-it-cool defiance—gone, upended. Sofia reached out, wanting to steady him, but the set of his jaw made it clear: he would break anything that tried to slow him.

She watched him pace, a caged animal searching for mesh to bite. He stared down the empty bed, the towel still wet on the rail, the ghostly persistence of her sister's routines—here and then, with a sickening click, not here at all.

"Maybe she left on her own," Sofia offered,

gently. "If someone knew she was waiting for you, she might've gone to ground—"

Julian cut her off with a gesture. "No. She'd never leave the research. Or the students." He kicked at the scuffed floorboards, a brittle, dry laugh bittering the air. "They took her. They said they would and they did."

Sofia saw the shape of his grief then, how it bent him. She searched the clutter for clues, reading the language of disarray: a trail of sand went to the back entrance, then out into the dense tangle of garden beyond. Rain had started in earnest, drumming on the old roof. She moved toward the sliding door, listening.

Rain spattered her face as she peered out. The trail disappeared quickly, washed away by the downpour. Turning back to the room, she allowed her eyes to absorb the details of Mila's life that Julian's frantic search had scattered across the floor.

"I'm calling Natasha," Julian muttered, already punching numbers into his phone. His voice carried the brittle edge of someone trying to maintain control. "Interpol has resources we don't."

Sofia nodded, her attention drawn to a bookshelf where marine biology texts mingled with dog-eared poetry collections. Sylvia Plath nestled between volumes on cetacean migration patterns. A small brass telescope sat on the windowsill, pointed toward the sea. Not just a scientist then—a dreamer too.

"I don't care about jurisdiction!" Julian's voice rose sharply. He paced the narrow confines of the room, one hand raking through his hair. "Someone threatened her directly. That's enough for an investigation... No, I understand protocol, but—"

Sofia tuned out his increasingly frustrated conversation, focusing instead on a collection of photographs arranged on a cork board above the desk. There was Mila —younger, laughing on a sailboat, her hair whipping across her face. Another showed her kneeling beside a tide pool, pointing something out to a cluster of local children. The joy in her expression was unmistakable, unguarded in a way the Vargas rarely allowed themselves to be seen.

And there, in separate frames, were her brothers. Josef in an expensive suit at some charity gala, his smile not reaching his eyes. Julian in what looked like Morocco, leaning against an ancient wall, that familiar half-smile playing on his lips. Both photos positioned at eye level, but on opposite sides of the board. Never together.

"Useless bureaucrats," Julian spat, ending

the call and shoving the phone into his pocket. "Natasha says they need more evidence of threat before mobilizing resources. A voice on a phone isn't enough."

Sofia moved to the kitchen area, taking in the collection of shells arranged by size on the windowsill. A half-finished watercolor of a humpback whale sat on an easel in the corner, the brush still in the water jar as if Mila had just stepped away for a moment.

"She left in a hurry," Sofia said quietly, "but I don't see signs of a struggle. No blood, no overturned furniture beyond what you just did."

Julian's jaw tightened. "That doesn't mean —"

"I know." Sofia held up a hand. "I'm just cataloging what we know. She packed a bag. She was making coffee but didn't drink it. Two sets of footprints leading out the back."

"So someone came for her." His voice dropped to something dangerous.

Sofia picked up a small glass figurine of a dolphin, turning it in her hand. "Or she left with someone she trusted." A pause and a thought. Sofia considered that someone else might have come through. Perhaps also looking for Mila.

She moved to a stack of notebooks on the desk, research journals filled with Mila's neat handwriting. Observations of whale pods, water temperatures, coral health. The most recent entry dated three days ago: *Juvenile humpback showing signs of entanglement. Will monitor tomorrow with Hiro.

"She wasn't planning to disappear," Sofia murmured, more to herself than to Julian. "She had work she cared about."

Julian had stopped his pacing, his attention caught by something on the floor. He knelt, picking up a framed photograph that had fallen from the wall. It showed a much younger Julian—perhaps twenty—with his arm slung around his sister's shoulders. They stood on the deck of a yacht, champagne glasses raised toward the camera. His face bore none of the careful control he maintained now; instead, his expression was open, almost reckless with joy.

"I'd forgotten about this," he said softly. "Dad's birthday. Before everything fell apart."

Sofia watched him trace the edge of the frame with his finger. It struck her suddenly how strange it was to be here, halfway around the world, chasing ghosts with a man she'd never intended to become entangled with. This wasn't a paid job. There was no client, no invoice to submit. She was here because Julian had asked, and she hadn't even considered saying no.

It was the sort of thing Nuno would do for her—drop everything and fly across continents because she needed him. The realization settled in her chest with unexpected warmth. It felt good to have someone to put first, someone to care for. But that same warmth twisted painfully as she watched Julian's face, haunted by the ghost of his sister's absence.

"We'll find her," Sofia said, the words emerging before she could analyze their wisdom.

Julian looked up, vulnerability flashing across his features before the mask slid back into place. "Yes," he said simply. "We will."

The storm outside intensified, rain hammering against the roof like impatient fingers. Sofia moved to close the garden door, pausing as something caught her eye.

Movement. She frowned towards the foliage.

Then, she went very still, staring. She stepped closer to the window, *listening* now.

In the rhododendron shadows, voices. Four, maybe five, low and intent. Boots squelching in the mud. Men—big ones, one with a smoker's cough and another who could have been a retired sumo by the shape of him. Sofia gestured at Julian, pressing a finger to her lips.

The men were coming straight for the house.

CHAPTER 2

"Julian, get down. They're coming towards us!"

But her fierce whisper was lost to him.

He didn't duck. Didn't pause. He put his shoulder into the door, opening it in one motion and strode straight out into the garden, every muscle in his body strung for violence, only the faintest tremor in his hand betraying the pressure inside. Sofia followed, a half step behind, scanning for weapons—not hers, but theirs.

At the edge of the patio, four men in black rain jackets, their faces set in the universal expression of hired muscle: mild irritation at being cold, wet, and in the company of people who might make things difficult. The tallest one—bald, with gold teeth and hands like canned hams—noticed Julian first. He muttered something in Russian, and the others tightened their formation, forming a crude wall at the top of the garden path.

Julian didn't slow down. "Where is she?"

His voice was a blade. "Where's Mila?"

The men looked at each other, a brief council of confusion, then the bald one shrugged and stepped forward. "You are Varga?" His accent was heavy, more Siberian than Tokyo. "We are waiting for you. We have message."

Sofia felt the spike of adrenaline in her ribs. She moved into Julian's line of sight, eyes flicking: two more men at the garden gate, one with a pistol visible under his coat. She filed their faces, their weapons, the heel-worn pattern in their boots.

"Who sent you?" Julian demanded, his English gone staccato. "Why are you here?"

The bald one showed a brief, gold-glinting smile. "Boss wants word with you."

"Where is my sister?" Julian repeated, louder.

A different man—smaller, with a twitchy left eye and a voice like wet gravel—interrupted. "You come now. No tricks." He eyed Sofia, suspicion sharpening his gaze. "Both of you."

Sofia met Julian's eyes, and in that moment she saw it: what he was about to do.

He stepped forward, right into the bull's-eye of the four men, and smiled. It was the old

Julian again, the wolfish charm reanimated by hatred.

"Where's my sister?"

"Funny," the Russian man said. "We were told to ask you the same question."

"Who sent you?" Sofia tried again.

But Julian clearly wasn't in the mood for collecting information. The heel of his palm was already moving. The sumo-sized thug noticed first and reacted with a shout.

But too late.

Julian moved with such lethal motion Sofia barely registered what happened next. One moment he was standing there, the next his fist connected with the Russian's nose—a sickening crack followed by a spray of blood that misted in the rain.

Before the man could even howl in pain, Julian had him by the nostrils, index finger hooked inside. The Russian went rigid, eyes bulging in shock.

"I've seen this done in Chechnya," Julian whispered, his voice eerily calm as he leaned close to the man's ear. "Special forces technique. One sharp pull and the cartilage tears away completely. Never heals right."

The Russian's companions lurched forward, but their leader raised a trembling hand. "Stoy! Stop!" he gurgled through the blood streaming down his chin.

Julian twisted slightly harder, and the man's knees buckled. There was something utterly transformed in Julian's face now—gone was any trace of the charming, brash man Sofia knew. This was something more primal—a predator with prey in its jaws.

"Where. Is. My. Sister?" Each word fell like a hammer blow.

"She was gone!" the Russian choked out. "When we arrived—I swear—she was already gone!"

Sofia wondered if these men were the source of the footprints.

The Russian's eyes darted to his companions, silently pleading for help, but Julian increased the pressure. "If you're lying to me—"

"Not lying!" Blood bubbled from the man's nose. "Your brother sent us to protect her—"

Julian's laugh was a terrible thing, sharp and humorless. He delivered a lightning-fast rabbit punch to the man's solar plexus. The Russian doubled over, wheezing.

Sofia noted how utterly unafraid Julian seemed. Four against one, and yet he controlled the entire tableau, wielding his body like a precision instrument. She'd seen him fight before, but never like this—never with this cold, calculated fury.

Movement at the edge of the garden caught her eye. Two more men appeared at the path's end, handguns drawn but held uncertainly. They hesitated, clearly unsure whether to escalate the situation further.

Julian didn't even glance their way. His indifference to the firearms was either supreme confidence or reckless disregard for his own safety—Sofia couldn't decide which was more terrifying.

He dragged the Russian by his nostrils toward the house, the man stumbling and whimpering as rain pelted them both. "Where is she?" Julian roared, his voice nearly lost in a sudden crash of thunder.

"Julian." Sofia stepped forward, her observational skills clicking into high gear. "I think he might be telling the truth."

Julian didn't release his grip, but his eyes flicked to her face.

"Look at their jackets," she continued, gesturing to the men. "They're not completely soaked through. They've been inside somewhere recently—the ferry terminal, maybe. They haven't been dragging Mila through this terrain."

She glanced upward as lightning split the sky, illuminating the garden in stark relief. The storm was worsening by the minute, wind whipping the palm trees into a frenzy, rain coming down in sheets so thick they distorted visibility.

"If they'd taken her in this," Sofia added, raising her voice over the howling gale, "they'd be drenched to the bone, covered in mud. They haven't been here long enough."

Julian's jaw worked as he processed her logic. The storm seemed to feed his rage, his hair plastered to his forehead, eyes wild in the half-light. "Who sent you?" he demanded, twisting harder.

The Russian gasped in pain. "Your brother—Josef! He wants to speak with you. He's looking for her too."

"Bullshit," Julian spat, but Sofia caught the flicker of uncertainty in his eyes.

In one fluid motion, he shoved the Russian backward into one of his armed companions. The men collided with a grunt, the gun clattering to the stone path. Julian scooped it up before anyone could react, leveling it at the group.

"Hands," he snapped. "All of you."

The men complied, raising their palms

slowly. The storm unleashed another thunderous roar, as if applauding the standoff.

"We go," Julian said to Sofia, never taking his eyes off his brother's men. "Now."

She nodded, edging toward the side path that would lead them down to the village. Julian backed away slowly, the gun steady in his grip despite the rain sluicing over his hand.

Once they reached the path, Julian lowered the weapon slightly. "Tell my brother if he wants to talk, he can do it himself. Not send his dogs."

With that, he turned and grabbed Sofia's elbow, guiding her swiftly down the treacherous, rain-slicked path. The storm had transformed the dirt track into a muddy rivulet, water rushing downhill with increasing force.

"We need to get to the research station," Julian shouted over the wind, tucking the gun into his waistband. "Someone there must know what happened to her."

Sofia nodded, struggling to keep her footing on the slippery descent. "You think Josef really sent them?"

She glanced over her shoulder, but the men were not following them, perhaps too scared of Julian to give chase.

Julian's expression darkened. "Josef doesn't do anything directly. But if he's looking for Mila too..." He left the thought unfinished, focusing on navigating the treacherous path.

The research station lay on the other side of the island, a twenty-minute walk in good weather. In this storm, with potential pursuers behind them, it would be a challenge. But Sofia saw the determination in Julian's stride, matching the fierce intensity of the gale that battered them from all sides.

Whatever had happened to Mila Varga, they would find answers—or else. The realization should have frightened her, this sudden, absolute commitment to someone else's cause. Instead, it filled her with a strange clarity as they pushed forward into the heart of the storm.

CHAPTER 3

The research station emerged through the curtain of rain like a mirage—a low cluster of buildings perched at the edge of a protected cove. Traditional wooden elements married with modern glass and steel, the architecture bridging centuries just as its occupants bridged worlds of science and local tradition. Solar panels gleamed dully on the main building's roof, while a small Shinto shrine stood nearby, its red torii gate vibrant even in the storm's gray palette.

Sofia noted security cameras positioned discreetly at the entrance—modern, high-definition, with motion tracking capabilities. The kind that recorded everything and missed nothing. Julian had already spotted them too, his gaze flicking upward as they approached the main entrance.

"Hiro will help us," Julian said, pushing wet hair from his forehead. "He's been Mila's research partner for years."

Sofia glanced at Julian. "I... I thought Josef and you said Mila was limping through life.

She worked small jobs... just getting by."

"In the summers," Julian began, paused, then amended. "She's improved. And this place... this place was an oasis for her."

He turned to look at Sofia, standing still for the first time in hours to hold her gaze. She could see the fear in his eyes. A fear he hid so well. Those same lonely eyes reflected the look she so often found when regarding a mirror.

He sighed and ran a hand through his sodden hair.

The rain traced rivulets down his angular face, gathering in the soft hollow of his jawline before dripping onto his worn corduroy jacket —the one with leather patches at the elbows that had seen better days. His blue eyes, normally so quick to crinkle at the corners with laughter, remained serious, troubled. The threadbare sweater beneath his jacket clung to his lean frame, holes visible at the cuffs where his long fingers worked nervously, a rare display of the anxiety he typically masked with charm.

"After our father died," Julian said quietly, "Mila was... destroyed. She couldn't eat, couldn't sleep. She'd call me at three in the morning just to make sure I was still breathing." He shook his head, droplets flying from his tousled brown hair. "It took her years to find her footing again. This place was the first thing that made her feel whole."

Sofia watched his face carefully, noting the tension around his mouth.

"She never believed Josef had anything to do with it, you know," he continued, voice dropping lower. "Even when the evidence pointed that way. The changed will, the business partners who suddenly wouldn't speak to us, the convenient timing." His laugh held no humor. "Mila would make excuses for him—said he was grieving in his own way, that he couldn't help being cold."

He looked away, staring at the research station through the sheeting rain.

"Sometimes she just wouldn't face hard truths. It was easier to believe in the brother she remembered from childhood than the man he'd become."

Sofia touched his arm gently. "People see what they need to see in family."

"Not me," Julian said, a hardness entering his voice. "I saw exactly what Josef was. What he is."

Julian turned back to the research station, leading the way inside.

Inside, the storm's roar diminished to a distant rumble. The reception area smelled of salt water, disinfectant, and green tea. A young woman behind the desk looked up, her professional smile faltering when she registered their drenched appearance and Julian's barely contained intensity.

"Varga-san," she said, recognition dawning. "We weren't expecting visitors in this weather."

"I need to see Hiro," Julian replied, not bothering with pleasantries. "It's urgent."

The receptionist hesitated, then nodded. "He's in the main lab. I'll show you."

As they followed her down a corridor lined with stunning underwater photography, Sofia absorbed details. Research schedules posted on bulletin boards. Staff photos showing diverse faces—Japanese, European, American. A whiteboard covered in neat kanji alongside English notations about tide patterns and whale migration routes. Everything spoke of meticulous organization and scientific rigor.

The main laboratory was a two-story space with floor-to-ceiling windows facing the churning sea. Despite the storm's darkness, the room felt alive with purpose. Researchers in white coats moved between workstations, some examining specimens under microscopes, others huddled around computer monitors displaying complex data models. Massive tanks lined one wall, housing various marine specimens in carefully maintained environments.

A man looked up from a central workstation—early thirties, slight build, with rectangular glasses and hair pulled back in a short ponytail. His eyes widened when he spotted Julian.

"Julian," he said, quickly setting down a clipboard. "What are you doing here?" His gaze darted to Sofia, then back, a flicker of apprehension crossing his features.

"Where's my sister?" Julian asked without preamble.

The laboratory seemed to quiet, other researchers glancing their way with undisguised curiosity. Hiro's posture stiffened slightly.

"I was hoping you would tell me," he replied, his accent more pronounced with tension. "She hasn't been here for three days."

Julian's face darkened. "Three days? And you didn't think to call me?"

Hiro gestured toward a glass-walled conference room. "Perhaps we should speak privately."

Once inside, Hiro closed the door and

sank into a chair, suddenly looking exhausted. "Mila asked for privacy. She said she needed time away from the project. It wasn't unusual —she sometimes takes solo trips to observe the southern whale pods."

"Alone?" Sofia asked, studying the researcher's face.

"Not entirely. Usually with Emi-chan, one of our graduate students." Hiro pushed his glasses up. "But this time was different. She seemed... distracted."

Julian leaned forward, hands flat on the table. "Distracted how?"

"Phone calls she wouldn't take around others. Late nights alone in the lab. She stopped joining our team dinners." Hiro's gaze dropped to his hands. "I asked if something was wrong. She said it was personal, nothing to worry about."

Sofia noticed the slight flush that crept up Hiro's neck when he spoke about Mila. More than professional concern there—something unresolved between them.

"Did she mention anyone threatening her?" Sofia asked. "Any unusual visitors?"

"No threats, but there was a woman." Hiro's brow furrowed. "European, very elegant. They spoke privately in Mila's office.

Afterward, Mila seemed... shaken."

"When was this?" Julian demanded.

"Last week. Tuesday, I think." Hiro hesitated. "There's something else. Two nights before she left, I found her in the specimen archive at 3 AM. She was photographing our historical records—logbooks from the old whaling ships that used this cove in the 1800s."

Sofia's interest sharpened. "What kind of records?"

"Navigation charts, mostly. Old hunting grounds that are now protected sanctuaries." Hiro looked troubled. "When I asked what she was doing, she just said, 'Sometimes the past isn't as buried as we think.'"

A commotion outside the glass walls interrupted them. A young woman had entered the lab, shaking rain from her jacket. Small and wiry, with blue-tipped black hair and multiple ear piercings, she moved with the coiled energy of youth. She spotted them through the glass and froze, recognition and something like alarm crossing her face.

"That's Emi," Hiro said, rising. "Mila's favorite student."

Before he could open the door, Emi was already backing away, turning to leave. Julian was faster, exiting the conference room in three long strides to intercept her.

"You know where she is," he said, not a question but a statement.

The young woman's eyes darted between Julian and Sofia, confused.

"Mila," Julian pressed. "My sister. You work with her."

"Worked," Emi corrected, her English crisp despite her nervousness. "Past tense. She left."

"Emi," Hiro said gently in Japanese, and Sofia didn't show that she understood, "these people are worried about Mila. If you know something..."

The student's posture softened slightly. She glanced at the storm raging outside, then back at Julian's face. Something in his expression must have convinced her.

"Not here," she said finally. "Too many ears."

She led them to a small equipment room off the main lab, closing the door behind them. The space was cramped, lined with shelves holding sampling gear, wetsuits, and underwater cameras.

"Mila-sensei wasn't herself these past weeks," Emi began, perching on a storage crate. "She was obsessed with the Kuroshio current shifts—how they're affecting migration patterns."

"That's her job," Julian pointed out.

"Yes, but this was different." Emi pulled out her phone, scrolling to show them a photograph. "She kept returning to this particular underwater formation. An old shipwreck, about three kilometers offshore."

Sofia leaned closer, examining the image —coral-encrusted timbers emerging from sandy seafloor, schools of fish darting through the skeletal remains of what had once been a substantial vessel.

"What's special about this wreck?" Sofia asked.

"Nothing, officially. It's been documented for decades—a 19th-century whaling ship. But Mila-sensei thought there was something else there." Emi's voice dropped lower. "Two weeks ago, she found something inside the wreck. She wouldn't show me what, but afterward, she started receiving those calls."

Julian's eyes narrowed. "What calls?"

"Late at night. She'd step outside to take them." Emi hesitated. "Once, I overheard her. She sounded scared, saying things like, 'I need more time' and 'They don't understand what they're looking for.'"

Sofia filed this information away, piecing together the emerging pattern. "And the woman who visited—can you describe her?"

"Tall, pale as porcelain. White-blonde hair cut very short." Emi's hands shaped the memory in the air. "Expensive clothes, but simple."

Julian and Sofia exchanged glances.

"When did you last see Mila?" Sofia asked.

"Three nights ago. She asked me to help her load equipment onto the research boat—diving gear, sample cases, more than usual for a solo trip." Emi looked down. "She made me promise not to tell anyone where she was going."

"Which was where?" Julian's patience was clearly thinning.

Emi pulled up another image on her phone—a tiny, uninhabited island barely visible on the horizon. "Kagami-shima. Mirror Island. It's protected—no commercial vessels allowed. Only research permits grant access."

"And that's where the shipwreck is?" Sofia confirmed.

Emi nodded. "She said she'd be back in two days. That was three days ago."

"We saw signs she'd been at her home only recently."

Emi winced, shaking her head. "Er, no... she had asked a couple of us to stop by, water the plants, that sort of thing."

"She told me she'd be here," Julian muttered. "She led me to believe she was still here."

Emi just shrugged. "Perhaps she was worried someone was reading her communications."

Julian considered, this and he shot Sofia a sidelong glance. She supposed she understood what he was looking for. Sofia had once been nicknamed the human lie-detector while at Interpol. She was watching Emi closely.

"Were you at Mila's place recently?" Sofia asked, studying the young woman's micro-expressions. "Yesterday, perhaps?"

Emi shifted her weight, fingers playing with one of her earrings. "Yes. I go every other day to water her plants while she's away." Her shoulders hunched slightly. "She has these orchids that need specific care."

"Did you notice anyone unusual around the property?" Julian leaned forward. "Men watching the place, perhaps?"

"No," Emi said, shaking her head

emphatically, though her eyes darted briefly to the floor—not deception, Sofia noted, but anxiety. "I didn't see anyone. I just went in, watered everything, checked the mail." She paused, brow furrowing. "I might have left a dish in the sink, though. I made tea and..." Her voice trailed off as she winced. "I'm sorry. I should have cleaned up better."

"It's fine," Sofia said gently. "We're not worried about dishes."

Julian ran a hand through his still-damp hair. "Did Mila say anything about when she'd return? Or if she was meeting someone at Kagami-shima?"

"No, but..." Emi hesitated, pulling out her phone again. "She did send me this yesterday."

She turned the screen toward them, showing a text message: *All good. Don't worry if you can't reach me for a few days. Signal poor here. Tell no one where I am. IMPORTANT.*

"Yesterday?" Julian's voice sharpened. "What time?"

"Early morning. Around 5 AM." Emi looked between them, confusion evident in her expression. "Is something wrong? Beyond her being late, I mean."

Sofia studied the text, noting the formal language that seemed at odds with how a mentor might message a student. "Has Mila ever asked you to keep secrets before?"

Emi's eyes widened slightly. "Not like this. We've had to be discreet about research findings before publication, but..." She trailed off, the implications of their questions finally sinking in. "You think something's happened to her, don't you?"

Julian's jaw tightened. "We need to get to that island."

"Impossible in this weather," Hiro interjected from the doorway, making them all start. How long had he been listening? "The storm's expected to intensify over the next twelve hours. No boats will launch."

"We don't have twelve hours," Julian snapped.

Sofia placed a restraining hand on his arm, feeling the tension vibrating through him. "Is there shelter on the island? If Mila is there, would she be safe?"

"There's an old research hut," Hiro confirmed. "Basic supplies, emergency radio. She would know to stay put in these conditions."

"Unless she's not alone..." Sofia murmured.

Julian was already moving toward the

door. "We need a boat."

"Wait," Hiro interjected, having listened silently until now. "The storm—it's too dangerous. The coastguard has issued warnings. No vessels are permitted to leave the harbor."

"I don't care," Julian replied flatly. "What's so special about a fishing wreck near whale pods? What would my sister have found that could've gotten her in trouble? Who was this European woman?"

Emi just shrugged. Hiro winced, shaking his head.

Sofia studied them and nodded a single time at Julian.

"This woman she spoke to," Julian said, "Did you get a good look at her?"

Hiro and Emi shared a look. "The security footage might've caught her," Hiro said. "But I'll have to get permission to show you. Might take a couple of hours."

"That's fine," Julian insisted. "But we need a boat, now. Any ideas?"

Hiro winced. "I... the storm's supposed to get really bad. Are you sure you want to do this? No one will take you in these conditions."

Emi bit her lip, her blue-tipped hair falling across her face as she looked down. "There's

Old Takeda-san," she said hesitantly. "He doesn't care about coastguard warnings. Says they're for tourists and fools."

"Where do we find him?" Julian asked, already moving toward the door.

"The south harbor," Emi replied. "The one behind the fish market. Look for the boat with the faded blue hull and the crane. But he won't do it for free, and he doesn't like foreigners."

Sofia nodded. "We'll manage."

"Wait," Hiro called as they turned to leave. He disappeared briefly into an adjacent storeroom, returning with two thick waterproof jackets and a sealed plastic case. "Take these. The jackets are thermal. The case has emergency flares, a satellite phone, and first aid supplies."

Julian accepted the items with a nod of thanks.

"I hope you find her," Hiro added quietly. "And when you do, tell her..." he hesitated, something unspoken passing across his features.

"Tell her what?" Julian pressed.

Hiro shook his head. "Just tell her to come home."

As they prepared to venture back into the storm, Emi caught Sofia's sleeve. "There's something else," she whispered, glancing around to ensure Hiro had moved out of earshot. "The day before she left, Mila-sensei asked me to download all her research files to an external drive. Everything on the Kuroshio currents, the pod migrations, the historical wreck surveys." Her dark eyes were troubled. "She said if anything happened to her, I should give it to her brother. The one who 'asks questions first and throws punches later.'"

Sofia felt a chill that had nothing to do with her rain-soaked clothes. "Did she say why?"

"No, but..." Emi hesitated. "She seemed scared."

CHAPTER 4

Outside, the storm had intensified, the wind now a physical force that pushed against them as they made their way down to the south harbor. The fish market was nearly deserted, most vendors having packed up early to escape the weather. Only a few stalwarts remained, huddled under plastic tarps, selling the day's meager catch to locals desperate enough to brave the elements.

The harbor itself was a study in battened-down preparation—boats double-moored, extra lines securing everything that might become airborne. All except one vessel. At the farthest pier, a weathered fishing boat rocked violently against its moorings, its blue paint faded to the color of a bruise. A wiry old man worked methodically on deck, securing crab pots as if the howling wind were nothing more than a mild inconvenience.

"Takeda-san," Julian called, his voice nearly swallowed by the wind. The old fisherman glanced up, his leathered face impassive beneath a salt-crusted cap. Deep creases around his eyes spoke of decades squinting against sun-glare and storm-spray alike.

"Go away," the man responded in Japanese, turning back to his work. "Harbor's closed to fools and foreigners. Today, you look like both."

Sofia stepped forward, addressing him in flawless Japanese. "We need passage to Kagami-shima. Immediately."

Takeda paused, weathered hands stilling on the rope he was coiling. His dark eyes assessed Sofia with new interest. "The research island? In this?" He gestured toward the churning sea, where whitecaps crashed against the breakwater. "Not possible. Not for any price."

"It's for Mila Varga," Julian interjected, stepping closer to the edge of the dock. "My sister. She's in danger."

A flicker of recognition crossed the old man's face. "The whale woman? With the laugh like temple bells?"

Julian nodded, rain streaming down his face. "She went there three days ago. Hasn't returned."

As he spoke, he looked troubled. Sofia could guess his thoughts. Mila had texted she'd stay put…

What if she hadn't been the one texting. What if someone had her phone.

Which meant someone had her.

Josef? Were the thugs lying about looking for Mila? It seemed unlikely. They hadn't been prepared for Julian. If they'd known he was going to be there, they might've come with more guns.

Takeda's expression remained stony, but something shifted in his posture. He tied off his rope then straightened to face them fully.

"Thirty thousand yen," he said flatly. "And if we die, I'll curse your ancestors."

"Forty thousand if we leave now," Sofia countered, already reaching for the ladder that led down to the rocking vessel.

The old fisherman barked out a sound that might have been a laugh. "You negotiate like a Kyoto wife." He gestured them aboard with a jerk of his chin. "The sea will collect the real price, not me."

The boat's cabin smelled of fish and decades of cigarettes—an oddly comforting combination that reminded Sofia of her father's old work jacket. But the thought of her father, especially while getting onto a vessel, only gnawed at her. She tried not to think of her parents. Their deaths. Of Valezzi.

One crisis at a time.

Takeda moved with the easy confidence of a man who knew every creak and groan of his vessel, firing up the engine without ceremony.

"Sit," he commanded, pointing to a bench bolted against the wall. "Hold tight. Bad crossing."

As they pulled away from the pier, the full force of the storm became apparent. Waves slapped against the hull like angry palms, sending spray across the windows. The boat bucked and pitched, fighting the current that sought to push them back toward shore.

Sofia braced herself against the wall, watching Julian's white-knuckled grip on the bench's edge. His eyes remained fixed on the horizon where their destination lay, invisible now through sheets of rain and sea mist.

"She's alive," Sofia said quietly, the words nearly lost beneath the engine's roar and the storm's howl.

"You don't know that."

"I do." Sofia held his gaze, reaching for his hand. It was an instinctive gesture, one that surprised even her as her fingers closed around his. His skin was cold and damp from the rain, but she felt the tension in him ease slightly at her touch.

Julian stared at their joined hands for a moment, then slowly turned his palm upward, allowing their fingers to interlock. The vulnerability in the gesture made Sofia's breath catch. This wasn't the confident, self-assured Julian who charmed his way through every situation. This was raw need—a drowning man grasping for something to stay afloat.

"My sister is all I have left," he said, voice barely audible over the storm. "The only family that still matters."

Sofia squeezed his hand gently. "We'll find her."

Sofia felt something shift inside her chest, a warmth spreading through her that had nothing to do with Takeda's overheated cabin. This wasn't part of their usual dynamic—the banter, the professional distance punctuated by moments of camaraderie. Always colleagues first, friends second, with that electric undercurrent they both pretended not to notice.

But this was different. Raw. Unguarded.

She looked down at their intertwined fingers, remembering all the times they'd worked together—passing documents in Venetian cafés, decoding messages in

Istanbul hotel rooms, planning extractions over Spanish tea. Always with that careful space between them, that professional buffer maintained by mutual unspoken agreement.

They'd saved each other's lives, yes. Patched wounds, shared safe houses, fallen asleep back-to-back. But never this—never this quiet, deliberate connection that felt like stepping across an invisible line.

Julian's eyes were fixed on the storm outside, but she could read tightness at the corners of his mouth, the barely perceptible furrow between his brows. Sofia had spent years training herself to read people.

But with Julian, it had become something else. Something dangerously close to caring.

He turned to her suddenly, those striking blue eyes meeting hers with an intensity that made her want to look away. She didn't. Instead, she found herself cataloging details she had no business noticing—the exact shade of cobalt darkening to navy around his pupils, the tiny flecks of silver near the outer edges, the way his lashes were unexpectedly long and dark.

Sofia tried to pull back mentally, to regain her professional distance. This was just comfort in crisis, she told herself. Just two colleagues supporting each other through another dangerous situation. Nothing more.

But the warmth in her chest disagreed, spreading with quiet insistence through her limbs, making her acutely aware of the rough calluses on his palm, the gentle pressure of his thumb against her wrist.

"What are you thinking?" Julian asked softly, his voice almost lost in the howl of the wind.

Sofia hesitated. Truth or deflection? The storm seemed to demand honesty.

"That I've never seen you afraid before," she answered finally. "It makes you seem..."

"Weak?" His mouth twisted slightly.

"Human," she corrected. "Real."

Something flickered in his eyes—surprise, vulnerability, and something else she couldn't quite name. Or perhaps didn't want to.

"I've always been real with you, Costa," he said, the familiar use of her surname a gentle tether to their established patterns. "More than with anyone."

The boat lurched violently as it crested a massive wave, sending them both sliding along the bench. Julian's arm instinctively shot out, trying to hold her, preventing her from slipping.

They tensed, both listening to the other breath, and then a massive wave crashed against the port side, sending a cascade of sea spray through a gap in the cabin window. The droplets caught in Julian's hair like tiny diamonds, trembling with each roll of the vessel. Outside, the sky had darkened to an ominous charcoal, clouds swirling in patterns that spoke of worse to come.

"Typhoon coming fast," Takeda called from the helm, his voice sharp with concern. "Forecast was wrong. Center moving this way now."

Sofia glanced out at the horizon where dark thunderheads merged with the churning sea. The line between water and sky had disappeared entirely, leaving only a wall of furious gray. Wind howled through every seam of the aging vessel, a banshee's warning of approaching danger.

Julian's fingers tightened around hers, and Sofia found herself holding on just as firmly. They sat together in silence as the boat fought its way forward, each crash of waves against the hull punctuating thoughts neither dared voice aloud.

"You two!" Takeda suddenly barked. "Come help! Now!"

The voice was like a starter pistol. It was

with some reluctance that Sofia released her hold on Julian.

Together, they rushed to the wheelhouse where Takeda was wrestling with the controls. The boat pitched violently, sending Sofia stumbling against Julian's chest. He steadied her with an arm around her waist, then moved toward the fisherman.

"Water in engine room," Takeda shouted, pointing to a blinking red light on his console. "Bilge pump failing. You—" he jabbed a finger at Julian, "—take wheel. Hold course. Woman, come with me."

As Julian took the helm, Sofia followed Takeda to a narrow hatchway. The old man handed her a powerful flashlight and pointed downward.

"Pump needs manual override. Green button, then count thirty seconds, then red lever."

Sofia nodded, descending the ladder into the pitch-black engine room. The stench of diesel and seawater hit her immediately, along with the ominous sound of water sloshing against metal. She swept the flashlight across the cramped space, locating the bilge pump against the far wall.

Above, she heard Takeda shout something unintelligible, followed by Julian's alarmed response. She worked quickly, finding the green button and pressing it firmly. The pump coughed, sputtered, then roared to life, but the sound was immediately drowned out by Takeda's renewed shouting.

"Boat! Following us!"

Sofia scrambled back up the ladder, emerging into the wheelhouse just as Julian pointed toward their wake. Through the rain-lashed windows, she could make out the sleek outline of a vessel cutting through the waves behind them—a modern yacht with a razor-sharp bow, its white hull gleaming even in the storm's gloom.

"Josef's men," she said, the pieces clicking into place. "They must have tracked us from Mila's house."

Julian's jaw tightened as he squinted through the rain. "That's not a local boat. Too expensive. Too new."

"Your brother's?" Sofia asked.

"Possibly." His eyes narrowed. "Or whoever sent those men to find Mila."

Takeda pushed past them, taking the wheel back from Julian with a grunt. "You bring trouble," he accused, glaring at them both. "Bad enough, storm. Now this."

Sofia turned to the old fisherman,

switching to rapid Japanese. "The sunken vessel near Kagami-shima—what do you know about it?"

Takeda's weathered face closed like a fist. "Old wreck. Nothing special."

"Then why is my friend's sister missing after diving there? Why are people following us?" Sofia pressed, bracing herself against the wall as the boat lurched through a particularly violent wave.

"Not my business."

"What about the whales? The ones Mila studies—have there been changes in their behavior recently?"

The old man's hands tightened on the wheel, knuckles whitening. "I fish. I don't track whales."

"A European woman," Sofia tried again. "Pale skin, white-blonde hair. Have you seen someone like that on the island?"

"No," Takeda snapped with sudden vehemence. "No foreigners except researchers."

The boat pitched sharply to starboard, a wave crashing over the bow with enough force to send spray exploding across the windows. For a moment, they were sailing blind, nothing visible but churning water.

"They're gaining on us," Julian warned, pointing at the pursuing vessel, now close enough to make out figures moving on its deck.

"Takeda-san," Julian called over the howling wind, "we need to outrun them. That boat—those people—they could be dangerous."

The fisherman spat a curse, then yanked the throttle forward. The engine roared in protest, the entire vessel shuddering with the sudden increase in power.

"Price just doubled," he growled. "Triple if we survive."

Sofia exchanged a glance with Julian. Why was Takeda so reluctant to discuss the wreck or the whales? If there was nothing unusual about either, why the obvious discomfort? Perhaps it was simply the timing. Too much going on. Stress, fear... it was why she'd asked the fisherman now—his guard down. But he was more scared of answering those questions than distracted by a typhoon.

Why?

The mystery of Mila's disappearance seemed to deepen with every question.

Through the rain-streaked windows, a dark shape materialized on the horizon—

Kagami-shima, its rocky shores emerging from the storm like the spine of some great sea creature. Relief washed over Sofia at the sight, but it was short-lived.

"They're still coming," Julian said, tension evident in every line of his body.

Behind them, the sleek yacht continued its pursuit, cutting through the waves with the determination of a jaguar with a scent.

"Do those men have guns?" The fisherman asked suddenly, peering wide-eyed through the storm.

Sofia spotted silhouettes moving on the yacht's railings. Were those flashes of light from muzzles?

Hard to tell.

"We need to outrun them," Julian said, grim. "Can you get us away?"

"Their boat is faster."

"Yes, but you're better, aren't you?" Julian insisted.

The small, Japanese fisherman puffed his chest in some pride. He didn't disagree and instead began barking orders once more. "Brace yourselves!"

Takeda spun the wheel hard to port, sending the vessel lurching into a narrow channel between two rocky outcroppings. The sudden maneuver nearly threw Sofia against the bulkhead. The old fisherman's face transformed, decades melting away as his eyes lit with a feral gleam.

"Hold tight!" he shouted, cranking another lever that made the engine roar like a wounded beast.

The pursuing yacht hesitated, its sleek bow hovering at the entrance to the channel where jagged stones lurked just beneath the churning surface. Their pursuer was faster, newer, but Takeda's weathered vessel had one critical advantage – a shallow draft that could navigate treacherous waters where deeper keels would founder.

"They won't follow. Too expensive to risk."

He was wrong. The yacht surged forward, its captain either reckless or desperate enough to chance the narrow passage. A wave crashed over their stern, momentarily blinding them with spray. When it cleared, the yacht had halved the distance between them.

Julian braced himself against the cabin wall, eyes fixed on their pursuers. "They're still coming."

"Then we go where they cannot," Takeda muttered, jerking his chin toward a nearly invisible gap in the cliffs ahead – a natural archway barely wider than their vessel, with the full fury of the typhoon's waves smashing through it.

Sofia's stomach dropped. "That's suicide."

"No," Takeda grinned, revealing tobacco-stained teeth. "That is local knowledge."

He cut the engine to half-power, timing their approach with the rhythm of the waves. The pursuing yacht was close enough now that Sofia could make out individual figures on deck – men in dark rain gear, one pointing what was unmistakably a rifle.

"Down!" Julian shouted, pulling Sofia to the floor as a crack split the air. The wheelhouse window shattered, sending glass skittering across the metal flooring.

Takeda didn't flinch. He waited, counting under his breath as a massive wave built behind them, then gunned the engine at precisely the right moment. The wave caught their stern, lifting the boat and hurling it forward like a surfer catching a perfect break. They shot toward the narrow archway, the rocky ceiling so close that Sofia could have reached up and touched it.

Behind them, their pursuers attempted the same maneuver, but their timing was fractionally off. The yacht crested the wave too early, its bow rising dangerously high before slamming down with bone-jarring force. A terrible grinding sound carried over the storm as the vessel's keel scraped across submerged rocks.

Takeda's boat burst through the archway into a sheltered lagoon, the water noticeably calmer within its natural breakwater. The old fisherman cut speed, turning to watch their pursuers through the shattered window. The yacht was limping now, listing slightly but still coming.

For a moment, Sofia thought they'd recover.

But the storm had other ideas.

As they watched, an enormous wave—at least thirty feet high—rose behind the vessel like a watery mountain.

"Rogue wave!" Takeda shouted, his voice cracking with alarm.

The wall of water crashed down on the pursuing yacht with devastating force. For a moment, the vessel disappeared entirely beneath the churning foam. When the sea settled, the yacht was listing badly to one side, its progress halted.

Takeda didn't waste the opportunity, pushing his aging boat to its limits as they approached the island's small research dock.

The wooden structure looked fragile against the fury of the storm, but it held as they bumped against it none too gently.

"Go," Takeda commanded as Julian secured a line to the dock. "I not stay. Find other way back."

"What?" Julian looked up in disbelief. "You can't leave us here!"

"Can. Will." The old fisherman's expression was implacable. "Storm getting worse. That boat—" he jerked his chin toward the damaged yacht in the distance, "—bad people. I know trouble when I see it."

Sofia stepped forward. "Takeda-san, please. We need—"

"Need to live," he interrupted. "So do I. Old man not die for strangers' problems." His gaze softened fractionally. "Mila-san good person. Hope you find her. But this—" he gestured at the raging sea, "—this too much risk."

Before they could argue further, Sofia grabbed Julian's arm. "He's right. We're endangering him by keeping him here." She quickly counted out the agreed-upon payment, plus extra, pressing the yen notes into Takeda's calloused palm. "Thank you for bringing us this far."

The old man nodded once, then turned

back to his controls. As they stepped onto the dock, the boat was already pulling away, disappearing into the curtain of rain like a ghost.

Julian stared after it, water streaming down his face. "Now what?"

Sofia shouldered the emergency pack Hiro had given them, turning toward the island's interior where a faint light glowed through the storm. "Now we find your sister."

CHAPTER 5

The research hut stood a hundred yards inland, a sturdy wooden structure built to withstand the island's frequent storms.

The rain lashed against them as they reached the structure, its windows dark and shuttered. Julian tried the handle, finding it locked tight. He circled the building, checking every entrance while Sofia sheltered beneath the narrow overhang, examining the structure.

"No lights, no movement," she observed. "The vegetation has grown up around the entrance—undisturbed for some time."

Julian returned to the front door, frustration evident in the set of his shoulders. "She said she'd be here." He rattled the handle again, then stepped back, assessing the building. "Stand back."

With one powerful kick, he struck the door beside the lock. The wood splintered but held. He kicked again, harder, his face a mask of determination. On the third attempt, the lock gave way with a crack that was swallowed by the howling wind.

They stumbled inside, dripping water onto the dusty floor. Julian fumbled for a light switch, but nothing happened when he flipped it.

"Power's out," Sofia said, retrieving a flashlight from their emergency pack. The beam cut through the darkness, revealing a space that told its own story—undisturbed dust coating every surface, cobwebs stretched across corners, the musty smell of a place long abandoned.

Julian stood motionless in the center of the room, water pooling at his feet as realization dawned. "She hasn't been here," he said, his voice hollow. "Not for weeks."

Sofia moved the flashlight methodically across the space—a small kitchenette with empty cupboards, a desk covered in papers weighted down by rocks, a narrow cot with a bare mattress. Everything spoke of absence, of plans interrupted, of someone who had left expecting to return but never had.

"She lied," Julian said, fury replacing shock. He slammed his fist against the wall, the sound echoing through the empty hut. "First she said she'd stay at her place by the research station... then she said she'd be here. Why would she say she'd be here if she wasn't?"

Sofia continued her inspection, professional instincts overriding emotion. "Maybe she couldn't tell you the truth, and maybe her student misunderstood... Maybe Mila was protecting you."

"From what?" Julian's laugh was brittle, dangerous. "I'm the one who protects her. Always have been."

The wind screamed around the building's corners, a high keening that matched the tension inside. Julian paced the small space like a caged animal, five steps one way, five steps back.

Sofia extracted the satellite phone from their emergency pack. "Let's call the research station. Maybe Hiro knows more than he was telling us."

Julian took the device, punching in numbers. After several tense moments, Hiro's voice crackled through the static.

"Julian? Is that you? Did you find her?"

"She's not here," Julian replied, his voice tight. "The place hasn't been used in weeks."

A pause, then: "She said she would be there... but she hasn't been checking in regularly." A pause, a smaller voice. "We've...

I've been worried."

"How long until this storm passes?" Julian demanded. "We need to search the rest of the island."

"I'm checking the forecast now," Hiro replied, his voice fading momentarily. "It's... not good. The typhoon has intensified. You're looking at another 24 hours at least before it's safe to venture out."

Julian closed his eyes briefly, frustration evident in every line of his body.

"Is there anything you found?" Hiro asked suddenly, his voice pitched higher with what sounded like genuine concern. "Has she contacted you at all?"

Sofia watched Julian's expression darken at the naked worry in the researcher's voice. Clearly, Hiro's feelings for Mila ran deep.

"No," Julian said flatly. "She's not here. No one is."

"I see. I've been trying her satellite phone every hour. Nothing. I thought perhaps..." He trailed off, the silence heavy with unspoken emotion.

Julian's jaw tightened. "We'll call if we find anything," he said abruptly, ending the conversation.

Sofia moved to the window, wiping

condensation from the glass to peer out at the churning sea. The lagoon where they'd entered was empty—no sign of the damaged yacht that had pursued them. "They're gone," she reported. "Either they've moved to another part of the island or..."

"Or they're already here," Julian finished grimly.

The hut creaked and groaned under the assault of the wind, the sound amplifying the sense of vulnerability. Outside, the storm had transformed the world into chaos—trees bent double, debris flying through the air, rain falling so heavily it seemed solid.

"We're going to have to stay put until this passes," Sofia said, turning back to Julian. "We can't search effectively in these conditions. We'd be risking our lives for nothing."

For a moment, she thought he might argue. The need for action radiated from him like heat. But then his shoulders slumped slightly, practicality winning over desperation.

"Then we use the time," he said, moving to the desk covered in papers. "We look for clues, for anything that might tell us where she really went."

Sofia nodded, relieved at his pragmatism. "I'll check the storage areas. There might be equipment, supplies—something useful."

They worked methodically, Sofia's flashlight beam illuminating corners while Julian examined the research materials left behind. The papers on the desk revealed themselves to be charts tracking whale migration patterns, with particular focus on anomalies in recent years.

"The pods have been changing course," Julian muttered, studying the maps. "Avoiding their traditional grounds near that shipwreck."

Sofia opened a closet door, the beam of her flashlight revealing shelves of scientific equipment. "Julian," she called, "look at this."

He joined her, examining the gear she'd discovered—complete sets of deep-sea diving equipment, professional grade and well-maintained. Behind them, tanks of air, regulators, underwater lights.

"She was planning serious dives," Julian observed, lifting one of the wetsuits. "These are rated for extended deep-water exploration."

Sofia's attention was drawn to a small waterproof bag tucked behind the tanks. Made of heavy-duty yellow plastic with a secure seal, it was about the size of a large paperback book. "What do you make of this?"

Julian examined it, turning it over in his hands. "Waterproof storage. Divers use them for equipment that needs to stay dry."

Sofia took it back, noting its weight—empty, but substantial in its construction. The material was thicker than seemed necessary for casual use, with reinforced seams and a specialized closure that could be locked.

Their search continued, revealing more research materials but few personal items. In a drawer beneath the narrow cot, Julian found a set of keys attached to a floating keychain shaped like a whale.

"Boat keys," he said, holding them up to the flashlight beam. "There must be a vessel somewhere on the island."

Sofia glanced toward the windows where rain continued to lash against the glass. "We could look for it, but in this weather..."

The decision was made for them as a particularly violent gust of wind slammed against the hut, the entire structure shuddering in response. A branch crashed against the roof, the sound like a gunshot in the confined space.

"Tomorrow," Julian conceded reluctantly. "We'll search tomorrow."

The temperature inside the hut had

dropped steadily as night fell, their wet clothes drawing heat from their bodies. Sofia shivered, wrapping her arms around herself as she continued examining the research materials.

"We need warmth," Julian said, his gaze falling on the small stone fireplace built into one wall. "There should be wood stored somewhere."

He located a stack of dry logs outside the back door, protected by a tarp that had somehow survived the storm's onslaught. Working quickly, he arranged them in the fireplace.

Sofia watched as he struck a match from the emergency kit, carefully nurturing the small flame until it caught the kindling. Within minutes, a respectable fire was crackling in the hearth, golden light pushing back the darkness more effectively than their flashlight.

"Swiss commando training?" she asked, impressed despite herself at the speed with which he'd created fire from nearly nothing.

A ghost of a smile touched his lips. "Camping trips, actually. Josef thought it would make me more presentable to have some traditional achievements." His smile turned sardonic. "He was disappointed when I enjoyed the survival skills more than the social connections for networking with the kids of other billionaires."

Sofia settled on the floor near the fire, the warmth beginning to seep into her chilled limbs. Almost unconsciously, she began to murmur under her breath—words in Russian, then Arabic, then Finnish, the familiar ritual calming her racing thoughts.

Julian watched her, his expression softening as he recognized the self-soothing technique. He sat beside her, close enough that their shoulders nearly touched.

"You do that when you're worried," he observed quietly.

Sofia paused, surprised he'd noticed. "It helps me think. Organize my thoughts."

"What are you thinking now?" he asked, the firelight casting his features in warm gold and deep shadow.

She considered the question, drawn to honesty by the intimacy of their situation—stranded together, the storm isolating them from the world. "That I'm afraid for your sister. That whoever was on that yacht might have her. That we might be too late."

Julian's face remained impassive, but she saw the flicker of fear in his eyes before he masked it. "Mila is resourceful. Stubborn. Like me." His attempt at lightness fell flat, but Sofia appreciated the effort.

"Tell me about her," she said softly. "Not just what she does, but who she is."

For a moment, she thought he might deflect, retreat behind his usual armor of charm and distance. Instead, he stared into the fire, something vulnerable emerging in his expression.

"She sees beauty everywhere," he said finally. "Always has, even when we were kids surrounded by ugliness disguised as luxury. Where I saw business transactions, she saw connections. Where I saw obligations, she saw opportunities." His voice softened with affection. "She used to sneak out of Josef's charity galas to watch street musicians, then come back and play what she'd heard on our mother's piano."

Sofia smiled, picturing a younger, freer version of the Vargas siblings. "You protected her."

"I tried," Julian said, his voice rough with emotion. "When our father died and Josef took control, he wanted to mold her into something she wasn't—the perfect society daughter, an asset to be leveraged in business alliances." His mouth twisted. "She fought him. Chose marine biology over business school. Chose real work over performative charity. But she never could quite leave him behind..."

"And you?" Sofia asked gently.

Julian's laugh held no humor. "I was the lost cause. The troublemaker. The one with the wrong friends and the right skills for Josef's more... delicate problems." He shrugged, the movement bringing his shoulder against hers. "It suited me. Still does."

Sofia felt the warmth of him beside her, a different heat than the fire provided. "You're more than what your brother made you," she said quietly.

Julian turned to look at her then, his eyes reflecting the dancing flames. "Am I?" The question held genuine uncertainty.

The moment stretched between them, intimate and charged with unspoken possibilities. Sofia found herself noticing details she usually forced herself to ignore—the curve of his lower lip, the faint scar along his jaw from some long-ago fight, the way his eyelashes cast shadows on his cheekbones in the firelight. They sat in silence, the crackling flames casting dancing shadows across the walls of the tiny hut as the storm raged outside, a world away from everything.

Sofia found her gaze drifting back to the fire, its hypnotic dance a welcome distraction from both the howling wind and the man beside her. The flames reminded her of Barcelona, of that rooftop bar where everything had changed—where a phone call had set them on this path.

She shivered, though not entirely from cold.

"What is it?" Julian asked, his voice low.

"Just thinking about how quickly everything changes," she murmured. "Three months ago I was in Lisbon, thinking I might actually settle down for once."

"You? Settle?"

"I almost had an apartment," she admitted. "With actual furniture I'd picked out myself, not just whatever came with the place."

Julian raised an eyebrow. "That doesn't sound like the Sofia Costa I know."

"Maybe I was tired of running." She poked at the fire with a stick, sending sparks dancing upward. "Valezzi's network is still out there. They sent that assassin after me in the countryside. Who knows what else is coming my way?"

The memory made her shiver again—the silent figure who'd nearly succeeded where so many others had failed, the bullet that had missed her carotid by millimeters.

"Cold?" Julian asked, mistaking her tremor.

She shook her head. "Just... thinking too much."

Julian shifted closer, his shoulder pressing against hers more deliberately now. The simple contact shouldn't have felt so significant, but it did—warmth and solidity in a world that had proven itself neither.

"You know," she said, the words slipping out before she could reconsider them, "I hate that I like this."

Julian turned to look at her, puzzled. "Like what?"

"This." She gestured vaguely between them, around the room. "Being trapped here with you. It's like..." She fumbled for the words. "Like I had to lock us both in this little bubble just to keep some warmth around me. As if it wouldn't choose to stay otherwise."

The moment the words left her mouth, she regretted them. They revealed too much, exposed nerves she usually kept carefully protected. She blamed the storm, the worry, the strange intimacy of firelight—she wasn't thinking straight.

"What are you saying?" Julian's voice had

dropped lower.

Sofia stared determinedly at the flames. "Nothing. Just a crisis crush. It's a documented psychological phenomenon—intense situations creating false emotional connections. The brain confusing adrenaline for attraction."

"A crisis crush," Julian repeated slowly.

She nodded, still not looking at him. "It's actually quite common in high-stress situations. The brain's way of—"

"Sofia." The way he said her name—her first name, not 'Costa'—made her finally turn to face him. His expression was unreadable, but his eyes were intent, searching hers.

"What?" she asked, suddenly defensive.

"Shut up."

Before she could respond, his hand was cupping the back of her neck, drawing her toward him with gentle insistence. His lips met hers, and the analytical part of her brain that had been analyzing details—the taste of salt from sea spray, the slight chapped roughness of his lower lip, the controlled restraint in his touch—fell suddenly, blissfully silent.

When he pulled back, his eyes were dark with an emotion that had nothing to do with crisis or convenience.

"I've been wanting to do that for a while," he said quietly. "Since Venice, if you want the truth."

Sofia blinked, momentarily stunned into silence. Venice felt as if it had been ages ago.

"That long?" she finally managed.

Julian's smile was small but genuine. "Longer, maybe. I just knew for sure in Venice." His hand was still at the nape of her neck, thumb tracing small circles against her skin.

Julian wasn't coventionally attractive. But his eyes mirrored hers. He saw the world in similar shapes. He'd lost his family. And in his case, it had been by choice. A brutal, cruel choice.

He'd been there for her again and again... He'd saved her life on more than one occasion. She'd returned the favor.

But most of all, she supposed she simply felt... at home with him. Not really... She had no home. But his presence was the closest it came. She didn't feel as if she had to keep it together, to remain composed and professional. Julian almost taunted irreverence from her.

His gaze dropped to her lips again, and this time when he leaned in, Sofia met him halfway. The second kiss was different—less tentative, more certain. His hand slid into her hair, dislodging the pencil that had somehow stayed secure through their journey. It clattered to the floor, unnoticed as Sofia's fingers curled into the front of his sweater, pulling him closer.

The wind howled outside, rain lashing against the windows with renewed fury, but within their small circle of firelight, a different kind of storm was brewing—one that had been building between them across continents and cases, through danger and triumph.

When they finally broke apart, Julian rested his forehead against hers, his breathing uneven. "Just so we're clear," he murmured, "this isn't a crisis crush for me."

Sofia found herself smiling, a genuine smile that felt strange and wonderful on her face. "No?"

"No." His fingers traced the line of her jaw with a gentleness that made her heart ache. "This is just the first time we've been somewhere without someone trying to kill us immediately."

"Don't jinx it," she warned, but she was still smiling. "Those men on the yacht might have something to say about that."

"Let them try. Right now, I'm exactly

where I want to be."

The admission hung between them, simple and profound. Sofia knew they should be focusing on finding Mila, on the danger that still lurked beyond their temporary shelter. But for this moment—just this one moment—she allowed herself to exist solely in the warmth they'd created together.

Tomorrow would bring its own challenges. The storm would pass, the search would continue, and reality would reassert itself with all its complications and dangers. But tonight, in this small hut on a forgotten island, Sofia Costa allowed herself something she rarely permitted—the luxury of feeling, without analysis or restraint.

She leaned forward, claiming another kiss, savoring the way Julian responded—like a man who'd been waiting far too long for precisely this moment.

Outside, the storm raged on, but inside, they had created their own sanctuary—fragile, perhaps, but for now, enough.

And yet, in the heart of a typhoon, gunmen were somewhere on the island. Mila was missing. And it all had something to do with a taunting phone call back in Barcelona, a change in whale pod patterns and a sunken ship.

CHAPTER 5

Sofia woke to a world transformed by violence.

Dawn's weak light filtered through the hut's windows, revealing a landscape ravaged by the storm's fury. Uprooted trees lay scattered like fallen soldiers, their massive root systems exposed to the air for the first time in decades. The path they'd followed from the dock had disappeared entirely beneath debris and standing water.

Julian stood at the window, his profile etched against the gray morning light. The fire had died during the night, leaving only cold ashes in the grate. They'd fallen asleep side by side, his arm around her shoulders, her head on his chest. Now, in the harsh clarity of morning, Sofia found herself wondering if the night's intimacy would survive daylight.

"It's still coming down," Julian said without turning. "Not as fierce, but steady. The wind's dropped below gale force, at least."

Sofia rose, stretching muscles stiff from

sleeping on the floor. She joined him at the window, careful to maintain a small distance between them. Outside, the island bore little resemblance to what they'd seen yesterday. The research dock had partially collapsed, splintered wood jutting from the water like broken teeth.

"No boats getting in or out today," she observed.

Julian nodded, turning to face her. His expression was unreadable for a moment, then softened as their eyes met. He reached out, tucking a strand of hair behind her ear with a gentleness that answered her unspoken question. Last night hadn't been forgotten or dismissed with the coming of day.

"I tried the satellite phone," he said. "Got through to Hiro. The damage is extensive everywhere—research station, harbor, village. He says it'll be at least two days before anyone can reach us."

Sofia processed this information. "Food?"

"There's a supply cache. Basic provisions, emergency rations. Enough for a week if we're careful."

She nodded, satisfied. "Then we continue as planned. We search the island for any sign of Mila."

Julian's hand moved to his pocket, extracting the boat keys they'd found the previous night. The little whale keychain caught the gray morning light, its blue plastic somehow cheerful against the storm's aftermath.

"I've been thinking about these," he said, turning the keys over in his palm. "If Mila had a boat here, it would have been moored somewhere sheltered."

Sofia considered this. "Not at the main dock—that's too exposed."

"Exactly." Julian's eyes lit with purpose. "There might be a cove, a natural harbor somewhere on the island's leeward side."

"The storm's still dangerous," Sofia cautioned, though she was already reaching for her jacket. "And those men on the yacht—"

"Might still be here," Julian finished grimly. "All the more reason to find Mila's boat before they do."

They gathered their supplies—the remaining emergency rations, flashlights, the satellite phone, and a crude map of the island Sofia had found among the research papers. Julian slung the pack over his shoulder, pausing at the door.

"Ready?" he asked, his eyes meeting hers

with an intensity that went beyond their immediate mission.

Sofia nodded once, resolute. "Ready."

The world outside was a study in destruction. They picked their way carefully along what remained of the path, navigating around fallen trees and debris. The rain had lessened to a steady drizzle, but the sky remained leaden, promising more to come.

They followed the coastline, keeping to higher ground where possible. The island was smaller than Sofia had initially thought—perhaps two miles across at its widest point. The terrain was rugged, volcanic in origin, with steep cliffs dropping to the sea on the windward side.

After an hour of difficult hiking, they crested a ridge that offered a view of the island's southern exposure. The sea was still angry, waves crashing against the shoreline. But there, nestled in a small, protected inlet, was a sight that made Julian pause mid-stride.

"There," he said, pointing to a narrow cleft in the rocks. Within it, barely visible from their vantage point, was a small dock and what appeared to be a boathouse built into the cliff face itself.

They descended carefully, the wet rocks treacherous underfoot. As they drew closer,

Sofia could see that the structure was older than the research station, its weathered wooden sides suggesting decades of exposure to the elements. The dock, however, was newer—reinforced concrete rather than wood, explaining why it had survived the storm intact.

Julian approached the boathouse door, inserting the key. It turned smoothly, the lock clicking open. Inside, the air was heavy with the scents of damp wood and the indefinable smell of the sea itself.

A boat was moored within—not the large research vessel they might have hoped for, but a sturdy, well-maintained rigid inflatable boat with an outboard motor. It bobbed gently on the sheltered water, secured to cleats on either side.

"It's not much," Julian observed, running a hand along the boat's side, "but it's seaworthy."

Sofia examined the vessel critically. "Not enough range to reach the research station in these conditions."

"No, but enough to get us to the shipwreck."

Their eyes met, understanding passing between them. The sunken whaling ship that had captured Mila's attention—the site she'd been studying obsessively before her disappearance.

"If she's not on the island," Sofia said slowly, "then whatever she found at that wreck might tell us where she went. Or who took her."

Julian nodded, his expression hardening with resolve. "There's diving gear in the hut. We could be at the wreck site in thirty minutes, weather permitting."

"The storm—" Sofia began.

"Is passing," Julian finished. "The worst is over. And every hour we wait is another hour Mila might need us."

Sofia couldn't argue with his logic, though caution urged delay. She remembered the urgency in Emi's voice when describing Mila's obsession with the wreck, the strange phone calls, the European woman who had left Mila shaken.

"Alright," she conceded. "But we prepare properly. Full diving protocol. Safety lines. No unnecessary risks."

Julian didn't seem to listen to the parts about safety and no risks. "Let's get the gear."

They returned to the hut, gathering the diving equipment they'd discovered the previous night. Sofia examined each piece carefully—the wetsuits were high-quality, designed for cold-water diving with additional thermal protection. The regulators and tanks had been meticulously maintained, the emergency flotation devices recently serviced.

"Mila takes her safety seriously," Sofia noted, checking the air pressure in one of the tanks.

"She always has," Julian replied, a hint of pride in his voice. "Even as a kid, she was the one with the first aid kit, the extra water bottle, the backup plan."

They loaded the equipment into waterproof bags, then made their way back to the boathouse. The rain had stopped entirely now, though the sky remained ominously dark. The sea had begun to calm, the waves less violent, though still substantial enough to make their journey challenging.

Julian started the boat's motor, the sound echoing within the boathouse like a heartbeat. As Sofia cast off the mooring lines, she felt a familiar tension building in her chest —the taut anticipation that preceded every dangerous undertaking.

They emerged from the sheltered inlet into open water, the boat rising and falling with the swells. Julian handled the vessel with surprising skill, navigating between debris that floated on the surface—branches, plastic, the detritus of human habitation swept out to sea by the storm.

"You've done this before," Sofia observed, watching his confident movements at the helm.

A smile touched his lips, though his eyes remained focused on the water ahead. "Summer job as a teenager. Boat tours for tourists in Greece. One of my many attempts to escape the family business."

Sofia tried to picture Julian as a young man, sun-bronzed and carefree, showing wealthy visitors the sights of Santorini or Mykonos. It seemed both fitting and incongruous—the easy charm that made him a natural guide, the restless energy that would have chafed against routine.

The shipwreck's location was marked on Mila's charts—approximately three kilometers offshore, in relatively shallow water for a deep-sea diver but deep enough to have preserved the vessel for more than a century.

As they approached the coordinates, the sea grew calmer, as if respecting the grave below. Julian cut the motor, allowing the boat to drift the final few meters. The surface here was different—smoother, with strange eddies that suggested unusual currents beneath.

"This is it," he said, checking the GPS unit

mounted on the console. "We're directly above the wreck."

Sofia peered over the side, but the water was opaque, its surface reflecting the leaden sky. Whatever lay beneath remained hidden, patient, waiting as it had for generations.

They prepared in silence. Sofia zipped her wetsuit closed, the neoprene tight against her skin. Julian checked her air tank, then his own, their fingers brushing as they helped each other with straps and buckles.

There was an intimacy to the process that transcended their night by the fire—a different kind of trust, born of mutual dependence in a hostile environment. If anything went wrong below, they would have only each other to rely on.

"The visibility won't be great after the storm," Julian warned, securing his weight belt. "We stay together."

Sofia nodded, attaching her dive light to her wrist. "Standard communication signals. If either of us gives the 'up' sign, we both ascend immediately."

They sat on the edge of the boat, fins dangling over the side, regulators in place. A final check of equipment, a last exchanged glance, and then they were rolling backward into the sea.

The cold was immediate and shocking despite the wetsuit's protection. Sofia felt her body instinctively tense, then forced herself to relax, to breathe normally through the regulator. The water was murky with silt stirred up by the storm, visibility limited to perhaps fifteen feet.

Julian appeared beside her, his form distorted by the turbid water. He gestured downward, then began his descent, Sofia following close behind. They moved through a world of muted sounds and diffused light, the pressure increasing gently as they dropped deeper.

At thirty feet, the water cleared suddenly, as if they had passed through a membrane separating two worlds. Below them, emerging from the gloom like a ghostly apparition, lay the skeletal remains of what had once been a proud vessel.

CHAPTER 6

The whaling ship rested on its side, its wooden ribs reaching upward like the fingers of a drowning man. Coral had claimed much of the structure, transforming utilitarian beams into sculptures of living stone. Fish moved through the wreck's empty spaces—bright flashes of color against the monochrome backdrop of decay.

Julian pointed toward the ship's bow, where the figurehead—a woman with flowing hair, her features softened by decades underwater—still gazed eternally forward. They swam closer, their movements awkward in the three-dimensional freedom of weightlessness.

The wreck was larger than Sofia had expected, at least 120 feet from bow to stern. Its masts had long since collapsed, but the main deck remained partially intact, creating a ceiling over what had once been the crew's quarters. Julian gestured toward an opening in the hull—a doorway perhaps, or more likely a breach through the wooden planks where decay had weakened the structure.

Sofia followed Julian as he navigated through the breach, their dive lights cutting through the darkness inside. The beam illuminated the remnants of the ship's interior—rotting beams, rusted metal fixtures, the ghostly outlines of what might have been furniture. Schools of tiny fish darted away from their intrusion, silver flashes disappearing into crevices.

The visibility worsened inside the hull, the water cloudy with suspended particles. Their lights created eerie tunnels of illumination, beyond which everything faded to murky shadow. Sofia swept her beam methodically across the space, searching for anything that might have caught Mila's attention.

Nothing seemed immediately unusual—just the expected decay of a century-old shipwreck. Yet Sofia couldn't shake the feeling of being watched. She glanced over her shoulder, scanning the water behind them. The Japanese waters near Okinawa were known for various shark species. Bull sharks, tigers, even great whites occasionally passed through these channels. Her training had taught her to maintain awareness, to never let the focus on the objective override basic survival instincts.

Julian gestured toward a narrow passage that led deeper into the ship's belly. The opening was tight—barely wide enough for their shoulders with the tanks. He positioned himself horizontally, easing through the gap with careful movements. Sofia hesitated, eyeing the constricted space. If something went wrong, extraction would be difficult at best.

Julian paused on the other side, looking back at her questioningly. She nodded, decision made, and followed his path.

Halfway through, her air hose caught on something—a protruding metal spike, rusted but still sharp. Sofia twisted, trying to free the tube without tearing it. The movement stirred up silt, further reducing visibility. Her fingers worked blindly, feeling along the hose to locate the snag.

Through the clouded water, a shape materialized—moving fast, a blur of gray and purpose heading directly toward her. Shark? Eel? Something large, certainly predatory. Pure instinct took over. Sofia yanked violently, freeing herself from the obstruction with a sharp jerk just as the creature reached her position.

She tumbled through the opening, momentum carrying her into Julian as a terrible muted sound reached her ears—the distinctive hiss of escaping air. Her tube had torn on the metal spike, bubbles now spewing from a jagged rip in the rubber.

The blur was gone, swimming back out into the water. But a more immediate danger presented itself.

Panic flared, bright and immediate. Without air, she had minutes at most. Julian hadn't noticed yet, his attention drawn to something ahead in the wreck's interior. Sofia forced herself to think, to recall her emergency training. Panicking would only increase her oxygen consumption.

She deliberately slowed her breathing, calming her racing heart. She pinched the torn section of hose between her fingers, creating a temporary seal. Water had already entered the tube—she had no choice but to swallow it, grimacing at the brackish taste that penetrated her regulator. The flow of air resumed, albeit reduced.

One hand now occupied with maintaining her lifeline, Sofia felt awkward, unbalanced—like limping underwater. She finned forward, catching up to Julian who was examining the far wall of the chamber they'd entered. The last time she'd been scuba diving had been in Hawaii, with two handsome hunks and an old friend who'd since inherited a billion dollar empire.

This venture was far less Bachelorette and far more Survivor.

Julian turned, gesturing excitedly at something she couldn't yet see. His eyes, visible through his mask, were wide with discovery. Sofia nodded, deliberately keeping her compromised air hose angled away from his line of sight. He was worried enough about his sister; her situation would only distract him from their mission. Besides, she was fine.

It was fine.

She hoped.

As she drew closer, Sofia saw what had captured Julian's attention. Fresh scuff marks marred the ancient wood and coral—bright scratches in the patina of age. Metal against metal, something heavy dragged across the wreck's floor. Recent activity, days old at most.

Julian pointed at a trail of marks leading to the chamber's far corner. Together they followed the signs of disturbance, Sofia moving awkwardly with one hand still pinching her damaged hose. The water resistance made maintaining her grip increasingly difficult, her fingers beginning to cramp from the constant pressure.

A small cloud of silt hung suspended near the floor, not yet settled—more evidence of recent activity. Sofia swam closer, her light revealing what appeared to be a rectangular outline in the wooden planking. A trapdoor, cunningly disguised but betrayed by the fresh scrapes around its edges.

She motioned Julian closer, indicating the discovery. His eyes narrowed behind his mask as he examined the door, running his fingers along its nearly invisible seam. Sofia could read his intention—he wanted to open it, to see what might be hidden beneath.

She began to move toward him when a shadow fell across them both, darkening the water as effectively as an eclipse blocks the sun.

Sofia turned, her light beam revealing a nightmare made flesh.

A massive shark—easily twenty feet long—hung in the water less than ten yards away. Its gray body was a masterpiece of evolutionary perfection, tapering to a crescent tail that moved with almost imperceptible undulations to maintain its position. Black, expressionless eyes regarded them with ancient hunger, its mouth slightly open to reveal rows of serrated teeth.

Time seemed to stop as Sofia stared into

those fathomless eyes.

The great white—for that's what it was, unmistakably—began to move forward, its massive body accelerating with terrifying grace directly toward her.

CHAPTER 7

Sofia's first instinct was to scream, but the regulator in her mouth transformed the sound into nothing more than bubbles.

The great white approached with the deliberate patience of an apex predator—no hurry, no wasted motion. Just inevitability wrapped in muscle and cartilage.

Julian spun at the commotion, his eyes widening behind his mask as he took in the scene. Without hesitation, he positioned himself between Sofia and the shark, arms spread wide to make himself appear larger.

The gesture was brave and utterly futile—like trying to intimidate a freight train with a stop sign.

The shark paused, perhaps puzzled by this strange new development. Its head swayed slowly from side to side, testing the water for scent, for weakness, for the electromagnetic signatures that betrayed fear and injury. Sofia's damaged air hose continued to leak precious bubbles, a beacon announcing her vulnerability to the ancient hunter.

Julian reached slowly for his dive knife, the six-inch blade laughably inadequate against twenty feet of evolutionary perfection. But his movement was steady, controlled—no sudden motions to trigger the predator's attack response.

Sofia fought every instinct screaming at her to flee. Running from a shark was like bleeding in front of a vampire—an invitation to become prey. Instead, she forced herself to maintain eye contact with the creature, to project calm authority she didn't feel. Her fingers cramped around the torn air hose, salt water continuing to seep past her makeshift seal.

The standoff stretched, measured in heartbeats that thundered in Sofia's ears. The shark's gills fluttered rhythmically, its pectoral fins adjusting position with minute precision. It was thinking—if such a word applied to a brain that had remained unchanged for millions of years.

Then, as suddenly as it had appeared, the great white turned away. Not fleeing, simply... losing interest. Its massive tail swept once, propelling it back toward the wreck's entrance with casual power. Within seconds, it had disappeared into the murky water beyond their lights, leaving only the memory of those black, emotionless eyes.

Used to humans?

Used to dangerous humans, perhaps? Had others been visiting this shipwreck frequently? She spotted healed scars along the shark's flank. Bullet holes? Harpoons?

It knew to leave humans alone... It had learned the hard way.

Lucky for them.

Sofia's legs trembled with delayed shock, her breathing rapid and shallow through the damaged regulator. Julian swam to her side immediately, his hands checking her equipment, his eyes asking questions she couldn't answer underwater.

She pointed upward—the universal signal for ascent. Julian nodded, understanding immediately that something was wrong. He positioned himself beneath her, ready to assist if her compromised equipment failed entirely.

They rose slowly, following proper decompression protocol despite Sofia's urgent need for surface air. Water mixed with air in her mouth, forcing her to swallow repeatedly to prevent choking.

Twenty feet from the surface, Sofia's grip finally failed. Her cramped fingers could no longer maintain pressure on the torn hose, and air began streaming freely from the rupture.

She had perhaps thirty seconds before the remaining air in her tank became inaccessible.

Julian saw the expanding cloud of bubbles and reacted instantly. He swam up beside her, removing his own regulator and pressing it to her lips. Sofia breathed gratefully, the clean flow of air a gift more precious than gold. Julian held his breath, his face calm despite the sacrifice he was making.

They buddy-breathed the remaining distance to the surface, passing the regulator back and forth. When Sofia's head finally broke through the waves, she gasped deeply, tasting the salt spray and storm-washed air with profound gratitude.

"What happened down there?" Julian asked, treading water beside her as she floated on her back, recovering.

"Air hose tore," Sofia managed between breaths. "And we had company. Big company. Great white. Twenty feet, maybe more." Sofia rolled upright, scanning the water around them. "It seemed... curious more than aggressive. But that could change quickly."

They swam toward their boat with steady strokes. Adrenaline provided the energy her body needed. As they reached the vessel, Julian hauled himself up first, then helped pull Sofia aboard.

She collapsed on the deck, exhaustion hitting her like a physical blow.

Julian knelt beside her, his hands gentle as he helped remove her mask and damaged regulator. "You should have signaled me immediately."

"You were focused on the discovery," Sofia replied, sitting up slowly. "I thought I could manage."

"The discovery." Julian's eyes sharpened. "Did you see the trapdoor? The fresh scrape marks?"

Sofia nodded. "Someone's been there recently. Days, not weeks."

"Mila," Julian said with certainty. "She found something down there, something worth hiding. Or worth taking."

They sat in silence for a moment, the boat rocking gently on the calming swells. The storm had passed almost completely now, leaving behind a world washed clean and strange. Sunlight struggled through the dissipating clouds, casting everything in shades of silver and gold.

"We need to go back down," Julian said

finally.

Sofia stared at him. "With a damaged air supply and a great white in the area?"

"I have backup regulators in the emergency kit. And sharks don't typically hang around wrecks during daylight. It was probably just investigating the disturbance we caused."

Sofia wanted to argue, to point out the dozen ways their second dive could go catastrophically wrong. But she saw the drive in Julian's face, the desperate need to find answers about his sister's fate. And despite her near-disaster with the shark, she felt the same pull—the investigative instinct that demanded resolution, regardless of personal risk.

"Five minutes," she said finally. "We get down there, examine whatever's hidden in that compartment, and get out. No extended exploration."

Julian's smile was brilliant with relief and gratitude. "Five minutes," he agreed.

As they prepared for their second descent, Sofia checked the sky for any signs of the storm's return. The clouds were breaking apart, revealing patches of blue that promised better conditions ahead. But she couldn't shake the feeling that the real storm—the one threatening Mila Varga—was just beginning.

The water felt different on their return, calmer but somehow more ominous. Sofia's new regulator functioned perfectly, but she remained hyperaware of every shadow, every movement in her peripheral vision.

The great white might have departed, but apex predators were rarely alone in these waters.

They descended directly to the wreck, bypassing the exterior examination this time. Julian led the way through the breach in the hull. Sofia followed, her earlier route now familiar, though no less claustrophobic.

Julian reached the hidden trapdoor and began working at its edges with his dive knife. The wood was soft with age and marine growth, yielding to his careful prying. Sofia positioned herself to provide light while maintaining watch for any returning predators.

The trapdoor gave way with a shower of debris, revealing a small compartment beneath. Julian's light beam penetrated the darkness, illuminating something that made them both freeze in astonishment.

Modern equipment. Waterproof cases, diving lights.

In fact, Sofia recognized some of the cases—made of the same material as the one they'd found back in Mila's research hut.

She tried one. Sealed shut.

She tapped Julian's shoulder and pointed at her watch. Their five-minute limit was approaching, and they'd already spent precious time examining the discovery. Julian nodded reluctantly, taking one of the cases and stowing it under his arm like a football.

With the waterproof case secured under Julian's arm, they began their ascent, leaving the ancient wreck and its secrets behind. The journey to the surface was mercifully uneventful, no massive predators materializing from the depths to challenge their retreat.

Back aboard their small vessel, Julian wasted no time. He placed the case on the deck, water streaming from its sealed edges as he examined the locking mechanism.

"Military grade," he murmured, fingers tracing the reinforced clasps. "Not standard research equipment."

Sofia knelt beside him, her wet hair plastered to her face as she studied the case. "Can you open it?"

Julian's response was a slight smile—the

confident expression of a man who'd never met a lock he couldn't defeat. He produced a small multi-tool from his dive kit and began working the mechanism.

The case surrendered with a soft click. Julian lifted the lid cautiously, as if expecting something to leap out at them.

Inside, nestled in custom-cut foam padding, lay a collection of objects that seemed wildly out of place in the modern world. Ancient coins, their surfaces green with age and corroded by seawater. Delicate porcelain fragments painted with intricate blue designs. A small jade figurine carved in the shape of a dragon. And most striking of all, a collection of folded paper packets sealed with red wax, the characters stamped into them faded but still legible.

"What is this?" Sofia breathed, reaching for one of the coins. It was heavy in her palm, the image of a long-ago emperor barely discernible beneath centuries of corrosion.

"These are... old. Very old."

"Edo period," Sofia said, recognizing the distinctive style of the porcelain fragments. "Maybe 17th century."

"Treasure?"

"Not just treasure. Look at these." She

pointed to markings on the inside of the case lid—modern notes written in a neat, feminine hand.

The handwritten notes were in Japanese—elegant strokes documenting each artifact Sofia leaned closer, her lips moving silently as she translated.

"Imperial collection... Tokugawa shogunate... official seal of..." She frowned, struggling with a particularly complex character. While she spoke Japanese, reading the language—especially handwritten—presented more challenges.

"What is it?" Julian asked, watching her face.

"These notes reference the Tokyo National Museum and Kyushu National Museum. There are catalog numbers, acquisition dates." Her frown deepened as she continued reading. "But there's something odd about the phrasing."

Sofia traced her finger along one sentence, translating slowly. "'Verification required—listed as displayed in west wing of Tokyo National but physically present in wreck site compartment.'"

"Museum pieces?" Julian examined the jade dragon with new interest. "But why would they be hidden in a century-old shipwreck?"

"These aren't just random artifacts—they're documented pieces from national collections. They shouldn't be here."

"Fakes in the museums, originals hidden away?"

"Or the other way around." Sofia carefully lifted one of the porcelain fragments. "The question is, who would go to such lengths? And why?"

Julian's expression hardened as he stared at the artifacts. "I want to see that security footage of the European woman," he said suddenly. "I want to see who my sister was so afraid of."

Sofia nodded, understanding his shift in focus. "The woman who visited the research station—tall, pale, with white-blonde hair."

"Someone who knew what Mila had found." Julian began repacking the case with careful precision. "Someone who didn't want these artifacts discovered."

"Or someone who wanted to ensure they remained hidden," Sofia added, helping secure the items. "There's more to this than simple theft. These pieces have historical significance beyond their monetary value."

The sun had broken fully through the clouds now, casting their small boat in warm light that belied the chill running through Sofia's veins. The mystery was deepening rather than resolving, each discovery raising more questions than answers.

"We need to get back to the research station," Julian said, securing the case with a zip tie from their emergency kit. "Hiro said the cameras might have caught the European woman."

Sofia glanced at the shipwreck site beneath them, knowing there were more cases waiting in that hidden compartment. More evidence, more clues to Mila's disappearance. But Julian was right—their next steps needed to be guided by understanding who they were dealing with.

"The storm's passed," she observed, looking at the clearing sky. "We might be able to make it back to the main island now."

Julian nodded, moving to the boat's controls. A small boat. Not meant for open water past the coast, but Julian wasn't in a patient mood. And Sofia knew that part and parcel of following the Swiss man's lead was embracing all things "risk."

And with his sister no closer to being found, it felt as if the clock was rapidly ticking.

"I wonder where our gunmen friends are," Julian muttered as he navigated the vessel out into open water.

"I'm not wondering at all," Sofia replied. "Wherever they are... I can't imagine they're up to anything good."

CHAPTER 8

The damaged yacht listed heavily to starboard, its once-gleaming hull now scarred by the typhoon's fury. In the wheelhouse, Aleksei Volkov pressed the radio transmitter with a thumb thick as a sausage, his scarred face set in grim lines as he delivered his report.

"No sign of Mila Varga yet," he said in Russian, his voice a graveled rumble. "But we tracked her brother to the research station. My men are in position."

Static crackled before a voice responded—cold, carrying the unmistakable edge of someone accustomed to obedience. "Your incompetence disappoints me, Aleksei. The delay is... problematic."

Volkov's gold tooth glinted as he grimaced. "The storm complicated matters. But we will deliver as promised."

"See that you do. Time is running short."

The transmission ended abruptly, leaving Volkov alone with the howling wind and the groaning protest of the yacht's damaged hull. He slammed his fist against the console, muttering a string of profanities that would have made even his former Spetsnaz commanders blush.

Below deck, six men waited in various states of discomfort. Dmitri, the youngest, leaned against a bulkhead, his face greened with seasickness. Two others cleaned their weapons, while the remaining three played cards, their expressions betraying nothing of the tension that permeated the vessel.

"The boss is unhappy," Volkov announced as he descended the stairs, ducking his shaved head beneath the low ceiling. "We move tonight. No more delays."

Mikhail, a wiry man with a puckered scar running from temple to chin, looked up from his cards. "The yacht won't make another crossing. Engine's flooded, hull's compromised."

"Then we swim," Volkov snapped, his patience as damaged as their vessel.

None of them noticed the slight bump against the hull—a sound lost amid the creaking of stressed metal and the persistent slap of waves. None saw the sleek, matte-black submersible that had approached from the island's blind side, using the storm's aftermath as cover.

And not one of the seven trained killers detected the figure that emerged from the water like a myth made flesh, scaling the yacht's side with the fluid grace of a creature born to both sea and air.

The first man died without making a sound. One moment he was checking ammunition stores, the next a blade whispered across his throat, parting flesh. His body was carefully lowered to the deck, blood pooling beneath him in a perfect circle.

The second and third fell together—twin knives finding twin hearts with synchronous thuds. They slumped forward over their card game, death masks frozen in expressions of mild surprise.

Dmitri, still nauseated from the storm, was turning when the shadow found him. His hand reached for his weapon but closed on empty air as steel punctured his carotid artery. His dying gasp was lost beneath the wind's mournful keening.

In the galley, the remaining two men sensed something wrong—the preternatural awareness of predators detecting a superior hunter. They moved back-to-back, weapons drawn. It made no difference. Death dropped from above, a lithe form descending from a maintenance hatch with impossible agility.

Limbs twisted, blades flashed, and two more bodies joined the growing collection.

Volkov was pouring vodka when he felt it—the subtle shift in the yacht's atmosphere, the primal awareness that he was no longer the apex predator aboard. He reached for his sidearm, but froze as he registered the figure standing in the doorway.

Slight, dressed in form-fitting black, face obscured behind a featureless mask. Not intimidating in stature, but radiating lethal capability in every line of their body. Blood dripped from twin blades, the droplets falling in perfect rhythm like a metronome counting Volkov's remaining heartbeats.

He fired—a desperate, instinctive response. The figure moved like liquid shadow, the bullet passing harmlessly through empty space. Before Volkov could adjust his aim, excruciating pain exploded through his wrist. He stared in shock at the stump where his hand had been, the severed appendage still clutching his weapon as it hit the floor.

The intruder produced a phone, tapping briefly before holding it up. A mechanical voice emerged from the speaker: "Where is Julian Varga?"

Volkov laughed through a grimace despite the pain, blood pumping from his severed wrist in crimson pulses. "You think I fear death?"

The figure tilted their head slightly, then tapped the phone again. The same question repeated: "Where is Julian Varga?"

"Kill me," Volkov spat, cradling his ruined arm. "I tell you nothing."

The assassin reached into a pouch at their belt, extracting a syringe filled with iridescent blue liquid. The needle flashed in the dim light as the assassin plunged it into Volkov's neck —avoiding the stump's desperate attempt to protest.

The effect was instantaneous.

Ice spread through his veins, a cold so profound it burned. Volkov's scream died in his throat as his vocal cords seized. The paralytic worked with terrifying speed, locking his muscles while leaving his nerves exquisitely, agonizingly aware.

The mechanical voice spoke again: "This compound affects only voluntary muscles. You remain conscious. You feel everything. In approximately three minutes, your diaphragm will paralyze. Breathing becomes impossible."

The assassin crouched before him, mask inches from Volkov's frozen face. A gloved finger traced the scar that ran from his left eye to his jaw—almost tenderly, like a lover's caress.

"Where is Julian Varga?"

Volkov's eyes bulged, the only part of him still capable of movement. His lungs burned, desperate for the air his paralyzed chest could no longer draw in. Black spots danced at the edges of his vision.

"Research station," he gasped, eyes fixed on the cash. "Western side of the island. He's searching for his sister."

The assassin nodded once, a single economical movement. The phone was tapped a final time: "Thank you for your cooperation."

Volkov's relief lasted precisely three seconds before the blade opened his throat in a precise, horizontal slash. He collapsed to his knees, hands futilely trying to hold his life inside his body as the assassin stepped past him without a second glance.

The figure moved across the deck with inhuman grace, stepping over bodies as if they were nothing more than inconvenient furniture. At the railing, they paused, scanning the horizon before slipping over the edge and disappearing beneath the waves.

Seconds later, a series of muffled explosions rippled through the yacht's hull.

Fire bloomed along the waterline, hungry flames consuming the evidence of the massacre aboard.

The submersible was already halfway to shore, its single occupant focused entirely on the next target. Julian Varga had survived longer than expected.

CHAPTER 9

Miles away, oblivious to the floating graveyard sinking beneath the waves, Sofia and Julian guided their small boat toward the research station's harbor. The water had calmed considerably, the storm's violence a memory written in floating debris.

"Something's wrong," Sofia said suddenly, her eyes fixed on the approaching shoreline. "The dock lights should be on by now."

Julian followed her gaze, noting the unnatural darkness of the research station. "Power outage from the storm?"

"Maybe."

They approached cautiously, cutting the engine a hundred yards from shore and drifting the remaining distance. As they drew closer, the silence became oppressive —no generators humming, no voices calling out, none of the normal sounds of a research facility recovering from a major storm.

"I don't like this," Julian murmured, securing their precious cargo of artifacts more firmly in its waterproof case.

Sofia nodded, her eyes scanning the shoreline for any movement.

As they beached the boat, the eerie silence pressed in. Sofia's skin prickled with warning. The research station loomed before them, its windows dark, reflecting the fading daylight like blind eyes. No movement, no sound except the gentle lapping of waves against the shore and the distant cry of seabirds.

"We should approach from the side," Sofia whispered, her voice barely audible above the wind. "Something's not right."

Julian nodded, securing their boat to a half-submerged piling. Together they moved up the beach, keeping low, the waterproof case containing the artifacts clutched tightly under Julian's arm.

They had nearly reached the building when Sofia froze, her hand shooting out to stop Julian. Voices—multiple, male, authoritative—drifted from around the corner. The cadence was unmistakable.

"Police," she breathed.

The voices grew louder, accompanied by the crackle of radios and the distinctive sound of tactical boots on gravel. Sofia peered around the edge of a garden shed, her breath catching as she confirmed her suspicion. Three officers in the dark blue uniforms of the Japanese Coast Guard moved methodically across the research station's grounds, powerful flashlights sweeping the area.

Julian pressed close behind her, his breath warm against her neck as he whispered, "What are they saying?"

Sofia listened intently, her mind translating the rapid Japanese. The words sent a chill down her spine.

"They're evacuating the island," she murmured. "Mandatory evacuation order. They're doing a final sweep to ensure everyone's gone."

"Why?" Julian's fingers tightened on her arm.

Sofia concentrated on the officers' conversation, picking out phrases through the gusting wind. "Something about downed power lines... unsafe conditions... potential fire hazard."

Julian's face hardened with resolve. "We need to find Hiro. He has the security footage of that woman."

"He would have been evacuated with the others," Sofia reasoned. "We should leave too, before they spot us."

Julian shook his head, a stubborn set to his jaw that Sofia recognized all too well. "Hiro cares about Mila. You saw his face when he talked about her. He wouldn't leave without showing us that footage—not when it might help find her."

Sofia wanted to argue, to point out the foolishness of evading law enforcement on an island they were trying to evacuate, but the determination in Julian's eyes stopped her.

"Fine," she conceded. "But we move carefully. If they catch us, they'll force us to leave."

They waited until the officers moved around the building's far side before darting across the open ground to a service entrance. The door yielded to Julian's touch—unlocked, another anomaly that heightened Sofia's unease. Likely, it had been left open in the station's haste to evacuate. Inside, the building was eerily quiet, emergency lights casting weak amber pools at intervals along the corridors.

They moved silently through the familiar hallways, heading toward Hiro's office. Sofia's senses were inventorying every sound, every shadow.

Hiro's office was empty, papers scattered across his desk. His computer screen glowed with a login prompt, the only source of blue-white light in the darkened room.

"He's not here," Sofia whispered, examining the space. "He left in a hurry. Evacuated probably."

Julian moved to the laboratory next door, finding it similarly deserted. Equipment had been secured—standard protocol for an evacuation—but personal items remained: a half-empty coffee mug, a sweater draped over a chair, a notebook open to a page filled with handwritten observations.

"The security room," Julian said suddenly. "That's where the footage would be stored."

Sofia nodded, recalling the facility's layout from their previous visit. "Lower level, near the main server room."

They backtracked, finding a stairwell that led downward. As they descended, Sofia heard voices echoing from below—more officers, systematically moving through the building, clearing rooms. Her pulse quickened as she calculated their options. If caught, they'd be removed from the island immediately, their chance to view the security footage lost.

"This way," she whispered, guiding Julian down a maintenance corridor that ran parallel to the main hallway.

The security room was tucked away in a corner of the basement, its reinforced door marked with warnings in both Japanese and English. Julian examined the electronic lock, a keypad requiring a six-digit code.

"Stand watch," he murmured, extracting a small multi-tool from his pocket. Sofia positioned herself at the corridor junction, her back pressed against the wall as she monitored both approaches.

Julian worked quickly, his fingers moving with practiced precision as he bypassed the keypad's outer casing. Sofia heard the soft click as he accessed the wiring beneath, followed by a series of beeps as he tested combinations.

In the distance, flashlight beams swept across intersecting corridors. Officers called to each other in Japanese, their voices echoing in the empty building.

"They're saying the west wing is clear," Sofia translated, tension coiling in her stomach. "They're moving this way. Hurry."

Julian didn't respond, his focus absolute as he manipulated the security system. After what felt like an eternity, the lock disengaged with a soft thunk. He pushed the door open, gesturing for Sofia to follow.

The security room was a small space dominated by a bank of monitors showing various areas of the research station. Most displayed empty corridors and laboratories, but two showed officers methodically checking rooms, moving closer to their position with each passing minute.

Julian settled into the chair before the main console, fingers flying across the keyboard. "How do I access archived footage?" he asked, frustration evident in his voice as Japanese characters filled the screen.

Sofia leaned over his shoulder, translating the menu options. "There—that one. 'Security Archives.' Then you'll need a timestamp."

Julian navigated through the system, following Sofia's guidance. "The student said the European woman visited last Tuesday. So... around midday?"

Sofia nodded, watching as he pulled up footage from the previous week. The system was complex, designed for professional security personnel rather than casual users.

"I need to search by location," Julian muttered, scrolling through options. "Where would Mila's office be?"

Sofia examined the building schematic displayed on a side monitor. "Third floor, east wing. Office 312."

Julian captured the image with his phone,

then used it to navigate the Japanese interface, matching characters on his screen to those on the system. His persistence paid off as footage began loading—grainy black and white video showing a corridor outside what must have been Mila's office.

"There," Sofia pointed as a figure appeared in frame. "That's her."

Mila Varga moved with the same fluid grace as her brother, though her body language conveyed a nervous energy absent in Julian's controlled movements. She kept glancing over her shoulder as she unlocked her office door, checking the corridor as if expecting someone—or fearing them.

Julian leaned forward, his breath catching as he watched his sister. "She looks scared," he whispered, his voice tight.

The footage continued, showing Mila entering her office. Minutes passed with no further activity. Then, at timestamp 12:47, another figure appeared at the far end of the corridor.

"That must be her," Sofia said, studying the newcomer. A woman, tall and slender, dressed in an elegant gray suit that seemed out of place in the casual research environment. Her white-blonde hair was cut in a severe bob that accentuated her sharp cheekbones and pale complexion.

Julian fumbled for the satellite phone they'd brought from the emergency kit, dialing quickly. "I need to call Hiro. He might know who she is."

As the phone connected, Sofia returned her attention to the door, listening for approaching officers. The voices were closer now, flashlight beams visible at the far end of the hallway.

"Hiro?" Julian's voice was low but urgent. "It's Julian Varga. We're at the research station."

Sofia couldn't make out the researcher's response, but Julian's expression darkened. "Where are you?" A pause. "I see. With the students." Another pause. "We're in the security room. I need the password to access the visitor logs."

Julian listened, his face revealing his frustration. "I don't care about the evacuation. This is about finding Mila." He waited, then: "Thank you."

Sofia heard it then—in the background of the call, a distinctive sound that made her blood run cold. A ship's horn, deep and resonant, signaling departure.

"Julian," she warned, "I think they're

leaving the island completely. That was a ship's horn."

His eyes met hers. "Hiro gave me the password. He's with the students on an evacuation vessel."

Sofia moved to the door, peering out into the corridor. Flashlight beams bounced off the walls, much closer now. "We need to go. They're almost here."

"Not yet," Julian insisted, already entering the password Hiro had provided. "I need to see who this woman is."

Sofia's heart pounded as she watched the officers' methodical approach. "Julian, they're coming. Now."

He didn't respond, his attention fixed on the screen where the footage continued to play. The blonde woman had reached Mila's office, knocking with deliberate movements.

"Damn it," Sofia hissed, making a split-second decision. She slipped inside the security room, locking the door behind her. "We have maybe two minutes before they try this door."

Julian barely acknowledged her, his focus absolute as the footage showed Mila opening her office door. The camera angle couldn't capture her expression, but her body language spoke volumes—the slight step backward, the tension visible in her shoulders. The blonde woman said something, then gestured for Mila to precede her back into the office.

"Can we get footage from inside the office?" Julian asked, fingers hovering over the keyboard.

Sofia leaned over him, navigating quickly to another camera feed. "Here—office interior cameras."

The new angle showed Mila's office—a cluttered space filled with books, marine specimens, and research materials. The blonde woman stood with her back to the camera, facing Mila across the desk. Their conversation appeared intense, the blonde woman's posture radiating authority while Mila's hands moved in agitated gestures.

"I need audio," Julian muttered, searching the interface.

A loud thump against the security room door made them both jump. Officers' voices came through clearly now, speaking in rapid Japanese.

"They're checking all rooms," Sofia translated, tension coiling in her stomach. "They have a master key."

Julian ignored the warning, his attention

fixed on the screen as he located the audio controls. Scratchy sound filled the room—just static.

Julian cursed. "Why can't I hear them?"

"Maybe the microphones weren't set up," Sofia whispered.

"Or maybe someone wiped them... but who would..." Julian trailed off, his eyes widening as he stared.

The woman had finally turned to face one of the cameras. Julian and Sofia both recognized her. She'd dyed her hair—or perhaps was wearing a convincing wig—but there was no mistaking her. Natasha Kovic. Julian's partner, and the woman who'd forced Sofia out of Interpol.

"Natasha," Julian breathed, his face draining of color.

Sofia stared at the screen, memories flooding back. Natasha Kovic—her former Interpol handler, the woman who'd orchestrated Sofia's dismissal. Tall, elegant, with a severe chignon and impeccable tailored attire. Those calculating blue-gray eyes and the small scar above her right eyebrow. The sociopathic genius who'd built her reputation on ruthless efficiency.

"What the hell is she doing with Mila?"

Julian's voice had gone dangerously quiet.

Sofia watched the silent interaction on screen, her mind racing. "Did you know about this? That Natasha was in contact with your sister?"

"No." The word was clipped, vibrating with fury. Julian's knuckles had gone white where they gripped the edge of the desk. "Why is she here? Why is Interpol involved with my sister? Unless..."

"Unless what?" Sofia pressed.

"Unless she's not acting in her capacity as an operative." Julian looked ghostly, as if he'd seen his own death foretold. "If she's gone rogue—"

Sofia shook her head. "That's unlikely. I know Natasha. She's cutthroat and icy, but the rules matter to her as much as anything. Structure. Protocol. It's her foundation."

Julian stared at her, conflict evident in his expression. After a moment, he nodded reluctantly. "You're right. Natasha's many things, but she's never been one to break rank. Which means..."

"This is an official operation," Sofia finished. "Interpol is interested in whatever Mila found."

A sudden pounding on the door

interrupted them—heavy fists slamming against metal, voices shouting in Japanese. The officers had found them.

"Open! Security! Open now!" The commands were unmistakable even through the door.

Sofia glanced around the small room. No windows, no other exits. They were trapped.

CHAPTER 11

The pounding intensified, accompanied by the metallic scrape of keys being tested in the lock. Julian stood, positioning himself between Sofia and the door, his body coiled with tension.

"When they come in—" he began.

"We surrender," Sofia cut him off firmly. "No resistance."

Julian looked like he wanted to argue, but another crash against the door silenced him. The frame splintered, hinges groaning under the assault. With a final, thunderous crack, the door burst inward.

Four officers charged in, weapons drawn, shouting commands in Japanese. Sofia and Julian raised their hands immediately, palms open toward the ceiling.

"On the ground! Now!" The lead officer's command needed no translation.

Julian hesitated, his muscles tensing. Sofia could read his calculations—four officers, confined space, he'd taken worse odds before.

She caught his eye and gave a slight shake of her head. Mercifully, for the first time today, he listened to her. His shoulders relaxed fractionally as he sank to his knees, then prone on the floor.

Sofia followed suit, wincing as rough hands secured her wrists with plastic zip ties. The officers were thorough, patting them down for weapons as they barked questions in rapid Japanese.

"Tourists!" Sofia cried in English, injecting fear into her voice. "We're just tourists! Please! We got lost during the evacuation!"

Her performance gave the officers pause. The youngest one looked uncertain, his grip on her arm loosening slightly.

"Tourists?" he repeated in heavily accented English. "Why you here? This area restricted."

"We were so scared during the storm," Sofia allowed her voice to tremble. "We got separated from our tour group. Please, we didn't know!"

The officers exchanged glances, their demeanor softening slightly. The lead officer spoke rapidly to his subordinates, gesturing toward the door.

For a moment, Sofia thought their ruse

might work. Then a stocky officer with a scar running through his left eyebrow spotted the waterproof case Julian had brought from the shipwreck. It lay partially hidden beneath the security console where Julian had stashed it.

Shit. The artifacts. Sofia's stomach dropped as the officer retrieved the case, setting it on the desk with a suspicious frown.

"What this?" he demanded, fingers working the latch.

"Just diving equipment," Julian offered, his voice carefully controlled. "We're scuba enthusiasts."

The officer ignored him, popping the case open. His eyes widened as he took in the contents—ancient coins, porcelain fragments, wax-sealed documents. Artifacts that clearly didn't belong in a tourist's possession.

"Sir!" he called sharply to his superior. "Look!"

The mood in the room shifted instantly. The lead officer crossed to examine the case, his expression hardening. He grabbed his radio, barking urgent commands in Japanese.

Sofia caught fragments of the transmission: "...suspected looters... historical artifacts... possibly connected to the museum thefts..."

Within moments, additional officers flooded the small room. Any pretense of gentle treatment evaporated as Sofia and Julian were roughly hauled to their feet. The zip ties were replaced with handcuffs, tightened to the point of discomfort.

"You are under arrest," the lead officer announced in careful English. "Theft of cultural property. Very serious crime in Japan."

They were shoved unceremoniously through the doorway and marched down the corridor, an officer gripping each arm with bruising force. Julian caught Sofia's eye briefly, his expression a mixture of frustration and grim determination.

This wasn't over—not by a long shot.

The artifacts complicated everything. What had seemed like a straightforward missing person case now involved international art theft, Interpol, and cultural treasures hidden in a century-old shipwreck.

And somewhere in the middle of it all was Mila Varga—marine biologist, Julian's beloved sister, and apparently, someone who had caught the attention of one of Interpol's most dangerous operatives.

The officers pushed them roughly onto the deck of a Coast Guard vessel, forcing them to sit on cold metal benches. As the engines roared to life, Sofia gazed back at the research station, growing smaller as they pulled away from the shore.

What had Mila discovered that had led to her disappearance? Where was she now? And most troublingly—if Natasha Kovic was involved, how much danger was she truly in?

The island receded into the distance, taking with it their best lead to finding Julian's sister. But as the boat cut through darkening waters, Sofia noticed something that sent ice through her veins—a sleek, matte-black shape breaking the surface briefly before disappearing beneath the waves.

Not a whale. Not a submarine.

A submersible. Military grade.

She blinked, certain she was just seeing things. But no, the water rippled.

What the hell... She glanced at Julian, but he was too distracted to have noticed.

She returned her attention to the rippling water. No more movement, no evidence anything had been there.

But Sofia knew what she'd seen.

A cold prickle crept down her spine. It wasn't the submersible that had her hackles up. Not exactly.

But the strange, spindly figure attached to the metal torpedo shape, like a spider clinging to an egg.

Someone else was hunting on this island.

CHAPTER 12

The mainland police station was a sterile expanse of fluorescent lights and hard angles, a stark contrast to the natural beauty they'd left behind.

Sofia's wrists chafed beneath the handcuffs. The room held only a metal table bolted to the floor and three chairs—two on their side, one across. The artifacts they'd recovered from the shipwreck sat in their case on a side table, now labeled with evidence tags.

"Any brilliant escape plans?" Julian whispered, his voice barely audible.

Before Sofia could answer, the door opened.

The man who entered seemed to bring winter with him. He stood perfectly straight, perhaps six feet tall, with the lean physique of someone who had spent decades refining his body through martial discipline. His suit was impeccable—white linen that should have appeared casual in the subtropical climate. A white handkerchief peeked from his breast pocket, folded into exact triangular points.

But it was his face that commanded attention. Pure white hair swept back from a high forehead, not the yellow-white of age but the pristine white of fresh snow. His left eye was normal—dark and sharp—but the right was milky white, the iris barely distinguishable from the surrounding tissue. A thin scar bisected his eyebrow above the damaged eye, continuing down his cheek to the corner of his mouth.

He carried a lacquered tray with an antique teapot and a single cup—no provisions for his prisoners.

"I am Inspector Takayuki Shirai," he said, his voice surprisingly melodic despite its coldness. He set the tray down and took his seat with deliberate grace. "I will be handling your case."

Sofia felt a chill that had nothing to do with the room's temperature. She'd interrogated enough people to recognize when she was in the presence of someone who had mastered the art.

This man was dangerous in ways that went beyond physical threat.

Sofia noted the details automatically: the way his fingers aligned perfectly parallel when he placed his hands on the table;

how his breathing remained controlled at exactly the same depth and pace; the absolute stillness of his damaged eye while the good one tracked everything. This wasn't just professional composure—this was something honed through decades of interrogation, a body language designed to unsettle suspects through its inhuman perfection.

Most tellingly, he hadn't asked them a single question yet. He simply sat, pouring tea into the single cup, allowing silence to do his work for him, creating a vacuum that most people would rush to fill with nervous chatter, with justifications, with lies that would betray them.

Shirai continued to pour tea into the ornate cup—a delicate piece of porcelain decorated with blue cranes in flight. The liquid steamed in the cool air as he raised it to his lips, inhaling the aroma before taking a measured sip.

"The typhoon has passed," he began conversationally, as if they were meeting for a social occasion. "Quite extraordinary, even by our standards. We Japanese understand typhoons differently than Westerners. We do not simply endure them—we incorporate them into our understanding of existence."

He took another sip, his milky eye fixed

unnervingly on Sofia while his good eye studied Julian.

"The word 'typhoon' comes from the Japanese 'taifū'—great wind. But its true meaning is deeper. It represents the impermanence of all things, the inevitable destruction that precedes renewal." His thin lips curved in what might have been a smile. "Rather like what has happened to you both."

Sofia remained silent, watching him. She'd encountered many types of interrogators in her career—the shouters, the friendly ones, the ones who relied on physical intimidation. Shirai was something different—a man who weaponized stillness.

"You have nothing to say?" Shirai asked, setting down his teacup. "Perhaps about the artifacts recovered from your possession? Artifacts that, coincidentally, match the description of items stolen from the Tokyo National Museum three years ago?"

Sofia kept her expression neutral, though her mind raced. Three years ago? That predated Mila's involvement entirely. Whatever they'd stumbled into went beyond Julian's sister.

"The typhoon," Shirai continued when neither responded, "has been most inconvenient for everyone. It delayed the evacuation order for Kagami-shima. An evacuation that was not, I assure you, due to downed power lines." He adjusted his cuff links—white jade set in platinum. "It was due to a police operation. One you interfered with most significantly."

Sofia caught the subtle shift in his narrative. Not a museum theft investigation, but a police operation specific to the island. She filed this information away, noting how Shirai's good eye narrowed slightly as he gauged their reactions.

"Theft of cultural artifacts is a very serious crime in Japan," he said, his voice dropping lower. "Particularly items of historical significance. The penalties are... substantial. Ten years minimum. Often more."

The threat hung in the air between them. Sofia studied Shirai more carefully now, noting details that told their own story.

"You're not regular police," Sofia said finally, breaking her silence. "Your suit is Brioni, not standard issue. The watch is Patek Philippe—approximately forty thousand dollars. Your teacup is Edo period, not something one brings to routine interrogations."

Shirai's expression didn't change, but something flickered in his good eye—surprise.

"Your right hand shows calluses consistent with traditional sword training—iaido, most likely, given your age and bearing. The scar above your eye is from a knife, not a blade—a street fight, not formal combat. You've moved beyond your origins, but you keep the scar as a reminder."

"Sofia," Julian warned quietly, but she continued.

"You're counterintelligence, not cultural preservation. Which means those artifacts are connected to something more significant than museum theft."

Shirai set down his teacup with deliberate care. "Impressive observations, Ms. Costa. Your reputation at Interpol was well-earned."

Sofia felt Julian stiffen beside her. Shirai knew exactly who they were.

"I find it curious," Shirai continued, "that a former Interpol analyst specializing in linguistic forensics and a man with Julian Varga's unique skill set would suddenly develop an interest in marine biology research and Japanese shipwrecks."

He reached into his suit jacket, extracting a thin folder which he placed on the table. "Perhaps it has something to do with Mila Varga's recent activities?"

Julian leaned forward slightly, the first sign of animation he'd shown since entering the room.

"Your file makes for interesting reading, Ms. Costa," Shirai said, opening the folder to reveal photographs, transcripts, and what appeared to be performance evaluations from her Interpol days. "Recruited at twenty-three. Specialized in detecting deception through linguistic patterns. Remarkable accuracy rate. Until your parents' deaths, of course."

Sofia kept her expression neutral despite the jab.

"And Mr. Varga," Shirai continued, turning a page. "Your file is considerably thicker. Former military. A billionaire's son who left his family's fortune. Then 'diplomatic security'—a convenient fiction. Your actual activities would fill several volumes, I suspect."

He closed the folder with a snap. "But what interests me is not your past, but your present. Specifically, your connection to stolen artifacts."

Sofia weighed her options carefully. Shirai clearly knew more than he was revealing, using information as bait to draw them out. The standard approach would be to remain silent, to give nothing away. But standard approaches rarely worked with exceptional interrogators.

"We found the artifacts by accident," she said finally. "We were looking for Julian's sister."

"Ah, she speaks," Shirai said, satisfaction evident in his tone. "And with a partial truth, how interesting." He poured himself more tea, the liquid steaming in the cool air. "Mila Varga has indeed been missing for several days. Though 'missing' may not be the correct term."

Julian's jaw tightened visibly.

"The research station reported her absence, but there was no formal investigation," Shirai continued. "Do you know why, Mr. Varga? Because your sister left of her own accord. After a most interesting conversation with an Interpol agent."

He switched suddenly to Japanese, his eyes fixed on Sofia. *"You understand what I'm saying, don't you?"*

Sofia hesitated only briefly before responding in the same language. *"Yes, I understand."*

Shirai smiled thinly. "Good. No time wasted then."

He returned to English. "Ms. Costa, shall we dispense with the pretense? You are not tourists. You are not scuba enthusiasts. You are searching for Mila Varga. I need to understand how deeply you're involved with the thefts."

"We haven't stolen anything," Sofia insisted.

"And yet…" He glanced at the artifacts.

"We uncovered those from a shipwreck," she countered. "Would you like us to tell you where?"

He blinked but didn't reply right away.

Julian had remained silent throughout this exchange, his expression growing increasingly stormy. But something shifted in his demeanor.

"Where is she?" he asked, his voice low and dangerous. "Where's my sister?"

Shirai regarded him with clinical interest. "That is precisely what I was hoping you might tell me, Mr. Varga."

"If I knew, I wouldn't be here."

"Perhaps," Shirai acknowledged. "Or perhaps this elaborate chase is part of a larger strategy." He gestured toward the artifact case. "Those items disappeared from the Tokyo National Museum three years ago. Their sudden reappearance following the *disappearance* of Mila Varga raises questions about your family's involvement."

Julian's eyes narrowed. "What are you implying?"

"The Varga family's business interests in Asia are well-documented," Shirai replied smoothly. "As are your brother Josef's connections to certain collectors who pay handsomely for items that cannot be acquired through legitimate channels."

Sofia watched Julian carefully, noting the slight whitening of his knuckles—the only external sign of his growing fury.

"My sister is a marine biologist," Julian said through clenched teeth. "She studies whale migration patterns. She has nothing to do with art theft or my brother's business dealings."

"And yet," Shirai countered... "The tide washes you into my interrogation room... So where is Mila? Is she involved? Was she your cover?"

Julian's restraint finally shattered. He slammed his cuffed hands on the table, the metal clanging loudly in the small room.

"Control yourself, Mr. Varga," Shirai said calmly, not flinching at Julian's outburst. "Such displays only confirm my suspicions."

Sofia noticed something in that moment —a slight hesitation in Shirai's movements as he glanced at the artifact case. His good eye lingered too long on the wax-sealed documents.

"You don't actually know where we found these," Sofia said, the realization dawning on her. "You know they were stolen, but you don't know they were in the shipwreck."

Shirai's milky eye remained fixed on her while his good eye narrowed fractionally—confirmation enough.

"Interesting that you immediately connected these artifacts to the Tokyo National Museum theft," she continued, leaning forward slightly. "Especially since we never mentioned where we found them. You've been searching for these items for three years, haven't you? But you didn't know they were underwater."

Julian watched now, letting her speak without interruption.

"Three years ago," Sofia said thoughtfully, "Julian and I were both active Interpol agents. We have documented alibis for our whereabouts." She smiled thinly. "You know this, of course. Which means you know we couldn't have been involved in the original theft. You're leveraging us because you're running blind."

A muscle twitched beneath Shirai's

damaged eye—the first genuine emotional response he'd displayed.

"Mila found something," Sofia pressed. "Something that connects to these artifacts. That's why Natasha Kovic visited her. That's why you evacuated the island—not because of the storm, but because you're searching for something."

Shirai's composure slipped further, his teacup clinking against its saucer with uncharacteristic clumsiness.

"The whale migration patterns," Sofia continued, the pieces falling into place. "They changed recently, didn't they? Avoiding that area near the shipwreck. Because it wasn't just a shipwreck—it was a drop point."

She gestured toward the waterproof case. "We found a similar case in Mila's research hut. Designed for deep-water retrieval. People have been using that shipwreck to exchange goods underwater, haven't they? A perfect transfer point—remote, seemingly innocuous, only accessible to those with proper diving equipment."

Julian stared at her, impressed despite the circumstances. Shirai's face had gone completely still, his damaged eye unblinking as he reassessed the woman before him.

"Who's been using it?" Sofia asked directly.

"A Japanese crime syndicate? Someone with connections to both the museum world and international smuggling?"

Shirai set down his teacup. "You are either remarkably perceptive, Ms. Costa, or dangerously involved."

"If I were involved," Sofia countered, "I wouldn't be asking you these questions. I'd already know the answers."

A long silence stretched between them, broken only by the soft hum of the air conditioning. Finally, Shirai exhaled slowly.

"The Inagawa-kai," he said, naming one of Japan's most powerful yakuza organizations. "They have been diversifying beyond their traditional revenue streams. Art theft provides excellent returns with minimal risk, particularly when the items remain in circulation among private collectors who ask no questions."

"But someone high up is protecting them," Sofia deduced, watching Shirai's micro-expressions. "Someone in law enforcement perhaps? Or politics? That's why the investigation has stalled for three years."

Shirai's good eye flickered briefly to the observation mirror—a tell that confirmed her suspicion. Someone was watching this interrogation, someone Shirai didn't entirely trust.

"We have... suspicions," he admitted carefully. "Nothing that can be proven. Yet."

"And Mila stumbled into this," Julian said, his voice tight with concern. "She discovered their underwater exchange point while studying whale migrations."

Shirai inclined his head slightly. "It appears so. Though whether by accident or design remains unclear."

"What do you mean?" Julian demanded.

"Your sister's research funding," Shirai replied, watching Julian closely. "It comes primarily from a foundation connected to your brother's business interests in Asia. The same business interests that have, on occasion, intersected with certain collectors known to acquire items through... non-traditional channels."

Julian's face darkened. "You think Josef is involved? That he's using Mila?"

"I think coincidences are rarely coincidental in matters of this magnitude."

Sofia watched the interplay, her mind racing ahead. "The European woman—Natasha Kovic. She's not investigating Mila. She's following up on her own investigation. Mila was an informant."

Shirai's expression remained neutral, but his silence was confirmation enough.

"Interpol has been tracking these thefts," Sofia continued. "They suspect the same high-level protection that you do. They approached Mila because she found evidence, physical proof they could use to bypass local corruption."

"A plausible theory," Shirai acknowledged.

"Is she in protective custody?" Julian asked, hope flaring in his eyes.

Shirai hesitated. "She would've been... but she disappeared three days ago." He released a sigh. "And you're not entirely correct, Ms. Costa. We knew these items were at a shipwreck. We'd narrowed the location to one of four. Mila Varga was helping us." He paused. "So where did you find them?"

Sofia considered the question. If Mila had been working with authorities, that changed everything. She needed to redirect this interrogation, gain some leverage, find a way out so they could continue their search.

"I'll tell you exactly where the wreck is," she offered, leaning forward. "But first, we walk out of here. No charges."

"That's not how this works," Shirai replied, his damaged eye fixed unnervingly on her face.

Julian had gone very still beside her. "Wait," he said slowly, "Interpol is working with you on this investigation?"

Shirai inclined his head slightly. "International art theft falls under their jurisdiction. They've been instrumental in tracking the network."

Something darkened in Julian's expression, a realization dawning that transformed his features from concern to pure, incandescent rage.

"Natasha knew," he whispered, then louder: "Natasha knew my sister was in danger and didn't tell me." A pause. An even bigger realization. "She's here… isn't she?" His head snapped up toward the observation mirror, blue eyes blazing with fury. "Get in here!" he shouted, his voice echoing off the sterile walls. "Natasha, I swear, you better get in here right now!"

Shirai rose smoothly, his hands making a placating gesture. "Mr. Varga, control yourself—"

In a movement too fast for Sofia to track, Julian's hands were suddenly free, the handcuffs dangling from one wrist. She blinked in astonishment—she hadn't even seen how he'd managed it.

"Julian, don't—" she began, but he was already on his feet.

Shirai's reaction was immediate and startling. With fluid precision, he flicked his wrist, and a slender blade appeared in his palm, materializing from somewhere within his immaculate sleeve. The knife gleamed under the harsh fluorescent lights, its edge wickedly sharp.

Julian moved with equal speed, catching Shirai's wrist before the blade could complete its arc. The two men froze in tableau, a deadly ballet suspended in mid-motion.

"You're making a serious mistake," Shirai said, his voice unchanged despite the strain evident in his arm. The knife trembled between them, neither man yielding.

Julian's strength was evident—his fingers whitening around Shirai's wrist—but the inspector's technique was flawless, his body angled to maximize leverage despite his disadvantage in raw power.

"Both of you, stop this!" Sofia commanded, rising to her feet despite her own handcuffs. "Julian, this isn't helping Mila—"

The door crashed open with such force that it bounced against the wall. Framed in the doorway stood a woman Sofia hadn't seen in months but would recognize anywhere.

CHAPTER 13

Natasha Kovic stood in the interrogation room doorway—her hair now black instead of the white-blonde from the security footage, cut in a severe bob that accentuated her sharp cheekbones. She wore a tailored black pantsuit that managed to appear both businesslike and vaguely threatening.

"That's enough, Julian," she said, her voice carrying the same icy tone Sofia remembered. "Release him."

Julian's grip tightened fractionally on Shirai's wrist before he abruptly let go, shoving the inspector backward. Shirai recovered his balance instantly, the knife disappearing back into his sleeve.

"You were there," Julian spat, advancing toward Natasha. "You met with my sister and didn't tell me she was in danger."

Natasha's expression remained impassive. "Your sister was a confidential informant in an ongoing investigation. Her safety depended on absolute secrecy."

"And now she's missing," Julian snarled. "How's that working out?"

Sofia watched the exchange, her mind recalibrating everything they knew. The wig on the security footage—Natasha had disguised herself, which meant she hadn't wanted to be identified. Not even by other law enforcement.

"Your sister isn't missing... or, well, wasn't..." Natasha said coolly. "She's in a safe house in Okinawa."

Julian froze. "What?"

"Or she was, until forty-eight hours ago." Natasha's gaze flicked to Shirai, something unspoken passing between them. "That's when she broke protocol and left our protection."

"Why would she do that?" Sofia asked, watching Natasha carefully for tells.

A flicker of genuine concern crossed Natasha's face before her professional mask returned. "Because someone contacted her. Someone who convinced her that remaining under our protection would put her brother in danger."

Julian's face drained of color. "Josef."

"We believe so. Though we haven't confirmed it."

Sofia studied the interplay between Natasha and Shirai, noting their careful positioning—too deliberate to be coincidental. They were partners in this operation, but there was tension there, something unresolved.

"You used her," Julian accused, his voice dropping dangerously. "You used my sister as bait."

"She volunteered. When she realized what she'd found, she came to us. Not the other way around."

"And you let her walk into danger!"

"We had her under surveillance," Shirai interjected smoothly. "Until the typhoon preparations made that impossible."

Sofia caught it then—the slight tightening around Natasha's eyes, the fractional shift in her stance.

"What aren't you telling us?" Sofia asked directly.

Natasha's gaze shifted to her former colleague, a cold assessment in her eyes. "There have been... complications."

"What kind of complications?"

Natasha's gaze cooled further, her lips pressing into a thin line. "We believe the Inagawa-kai may have taken her."

Julian's face contorted with rage. "The yakuza? And you're just telling me this now?"

"It's a working theory," Inspector Shirai interjected. "We don't have confirmation."

Natasha nodded. "It makes the most sense. They discovered she was cooperating with us. Who else would have the resources to track her to a secure location?"

Sofia leaned forward. "But you said she left voluntarily. That doesn't sound like a kidnapping."

"She was lured out," Natasha replied, her voice taking on an edge of frustration. "Someone sent messages claiming Julian was in danger. We intercepted the texts on her phone, but the trail went cold. We couldn't trace the origin."

"Anyone could have sent those texts," Sofia pointed out, studying Natasha's face for deception. "There's no evidence linking them specifically to the yakuza."

"We have reason to believe—"

"What reason?" Sofia pressed, recognizing the evasion tactic she'd seen Natasha use countless times during their Interpol days. "What actual evidence connects them to Mila's disappearance?"

Natasha's jaw tightened almost

imperceptibly. "Cell tower triangulation places her last known location near a property with known Inagawa-kai connections."

"That's circumstantial at best," Sofia countered.

Natasha waved away the objection with a dismissive flick of her wrist. "Regardless of your assessment, we have an operation planned for tonight. Our informant has identified a meeting of high-ranking Inagawa-kai members at a private club in Naha. If Mila is being held, someone there will know where."

Sofia watched as understanding dawned on Julian's face—the same realization that had just crystallized in her own mind. This wasn't about finding Mila. This was about using Julian.

"You want me to go in," Julian said, his voice flat with certainty.

"You have skills that would be valuable in this operation," Natasha replied coolly. "And motivation to ensure its success."

Sofia felt fury building in her chest, hot and dangerous. "This is a setup. You're using Mila's disappearance to insert Julian into an operation you've probably been planning for months."

"Don't be dramatic, Sofia. This is about

finding Mila and breaking open a major criminal enterprise. Julian's participation simply... aligns multiple interests."

"I'll do it," Julian interrupted, his gaze fixed on Natasha.

"Julian," Sofia protested, turning to face him. "They're manipulating you."

"I know exactly what they're doing. And I don't care. If there's any chance Mila is there—any chance at all—I'm going in."

Sofia stared at him, recognizing the stubborn set of his jaw. He knew he was being used. He knew the risks. And he was walking into them anyway, eyes wide open, because the alternative—doing nothing while Mila remained missing—was unthinkable to him.

"Excellent," Natasha said, satisfaction evident in her tone. "Inspector Shirai will brief you on the operational details."

Sofia turned slowly to face her former colleague, not bothering to mask the contempt in her expression. Natasha met her gaze without flinching, ice meeting fire across the small interrogation room.

"And me?" Sofia asked, though she already knew the answer.

"You'll remain here. For your own safety, of course."

"Of course," Sofia echoed, her voice dripping with sarcasm.

Shirai moved toward the door, gesturing for Julian to follow. "We should begin preparations immediately. The window of opportunity is narrow."

Julian hesitated, glancing back at Sofia. Something passed between them—an unspoken acknowledgment of what had begun in that storm-battered hut, a connection too new and fragile to name.

"I'll be fine," he said quietly. "This isn't my first dangerous operation."

Sofia wanted to argue, to point out all the ways this could go catastrophically wrong, but she recognized the futility. Julian had made his decision. Instead, she nodded once, sharply.

"Be careful," she said simply.

As Julian followed Shirai from the room, Sofia turned back to Natasha, who remained standing by the observation window, her posture perfect, her expression unreadable.

"If anything happens to him," Sofia said, her voice low and dangerous, "there won't be a place on earth where you can hide from me."

Natasha's lips curved in a cold smile. "Still so emotional, Sofia. It's why you never quite fit at Interpol."

"No," Sofia countered, stepping closer. "I never quite fit because I couldn't stomach using people the way you do. Treating them like pieces on a chessboard."

"Sometimes sacrifices must be made for the greater good."

"And sometimes, people use the greater good to justify their own ambition."

Something flickered in Natasha's eyes—a momentary crack in her perfect façade. Then she turned away, moving toward the door with measured steps.

"Get comfortable," she advised without looking back. "It's going to be a long night."

As the door closed behind her, Sofia sank back into her chair, mind racing. Julian was walking into danger, Mila remained missing, and somewhere in the tangle of art theft, yakuza operations, and international investigations lay answers that might save them both.

She glanced at the observation mirror, knowing someone likely still watched from beyond.

Sofia began to murmur softly, words flowing in a dozen languages—Russian, Arabic, Japanese, Greek—the familiar ritual helping to order her thoughts, to calm the fury and fear threatening to overwhelm her focus.

She needed a plan. And quickly.

Because whatever Natasha had claimed, Sofia knew one thing with absolute certainty: Julian would need her before the night was through.

CHAPTER 14

The alley behind the Jade Dragon club reeked of fish sauce and cigarettes. Julian pressed his back against the damp concrete, counting the seconds between security patrols. Three guards had passed already.

Fifteen seconds. Twenty. The next guard would appear in five, four, three...

Right on schedule, a burly man with neck tattoos peeking above his collar rounded the corner. Julian remained motionless, controlling his breathing until it was nearly imperceptible. The guard passed within inches, never sensing the predator in his shadow.

The moment the guard disappeared, Julian moved. Fluid, silent, he scaled the drainage pipe to the second-floor window Natasha had identified as a blind spot in their security cameras. His fingers found purchase in crevices invisible to untrained eyes, his body remembering skills honed through years of covert operations.

The window yielded to his glass cutter—a perfect circle just large enough to reach through and disengage the lock. No alarm triggered. No sound beyond the whisper of the night breeze. Julian slipped inside, becoming one with the darkness.

***

They moved like ink through water, their black-clad form barely disturbing the air as they navigated the ventilation shaft above the police station's main corridor.

The compound below buzzed with activity—officers changing shifts, paperwork being processed, the mundane machinery of law enforcement grinding onward, oblivious to the death sliding silently overhead.

Through a vent grate, they watched an officer deliver coffee to the security desk. Three personnel monitored the surveillance feeds. Two more guarded the corridor leading to the high-security wing where Sofia Costa was being held.

They tested the grate—secured with four screws, recently tightened. No matter. From a pouch at their waist, they extracted a tool older than any modern security system—a set of finger claws fashioned from blackened steel, each ending in a point that could pierce flesh as easily as metal.

They loosened each screw, catching them before they could fall and alert those below. When the grate was free, they replaced it in its frame, leaving it seemingly undisturbed. Patience. The moment would come.

***

Julian ghosted through the opulent hallway, his steps falling between the floorboards' pressure points. The yakuza headquarters disguised itself as a high-end club, but the upper floors revealed its true purpose—lacquered screens depicting ancient battles, priceless artifacts displayed in glass cases, security that would make most embassies envious.

A door opened ahead.

Julian melted into a recessed doorway, becoming part of the shadows as two men passed. Their conversation drifted to him in fragments of Japanese—discussions of shipments, payments, a problem that needed solving.

When they mentioned a foreign woman, Julian's muscles tensed, but his face remained impassive. Mila? Perhaps. His Japanese wasn't like Sofia's.

The thought of Sofia felt like a gut punch, tugging at his stomach, but he forced it aside. He couldn't afford to let it weigh on him. Not now. Not yet.

Only the target. He had to compartmentalize. Had to focus solely on the target.

He continued his advance, passing through the building like a ghost. Three floors up, past guards who would later swear no one had entered, Julian found himself in a corridor lined with traditional Japanese artwork. At its end stood an ornate door guarded by a single man—unusual for a security-obsessed organization, unless what lay beyond was known only to a select few.

Julian assessed the guard—mid-thirties, military bearing, a subtle bulge beneath his suit jacket indicating a shoulder holster. Experienced, but not exceptional. Julian reached into his pocket, extracting a small metal object no larger than a coin. He flicked it down the hallway, the soft clink drawing the guard's attention for just a moment.

A moment was all he needed.

***

They dropped from the ceiling vent in a controlled fall, landing in perfect silence behind the desk sergeant who monitored the security feeds.

The man never sensed their presence—

one heartbeat he was alone, the next a garrote wire slipped around his throat, cutting off both air and sound.

They lowered his body gently, arranging him as if he had simply dozed off at his post. The security monitors continued their silent display—hallways, cells, processing areas. There—the third screen from the left showed a woman sitting alone in an interrogation room, her dark hair falling forward as she worked at something in her lap.

Sofia Costa. Former Interpol. Current obstacle.

They moved toward the corridor leading to the high-security wing, extracting two slender blades from sheaths strapped to their thighs. The weapons were ancient in design but modern in composition—ceramic composite that would pass through any metal detector, sharp enough to slice through bone with minimal resistance.

Two guards stood at the security checkpoint, their attention focused on a tablet displaying what appeared to be sports highlights. Amateurs. They would never see another game.

***

The guard crumpled without a sound, Julian's forearm locked around his throat in a blood choke that induced unconsciousness in seconds. He dragged the man into a nearby alcove, securing him with his own tie and belt. The guard would wake with a headache but nothing worse—Julian wasn't here for unnecessary killing.

The ornate door yielded to the guard's keycard. Julian slipped inside, finding himself in a traditional Japanese study. Tatami mats covered the floor, scrolls depicting ancient battles hung on the walls, and a low table held an antique tea set.

Behind the table sat a man in his sixties, his silver hair pulled back in a severe style that emphasized the sharp angles of his face.

Five men flanked the figure behind the table.

The men saw Julian immediately. No subterfuge would work now.

Julian assessed his opponents in the split second before violence erupted—two carried visible weapons, the others would be armed as well. The silver-haired man behind the table hadn't moved, his obsidian eyes watching with detached interest.

"Forgive the intrusion," Julian said in Japanese, his pronunciation sloppy, hinting at his limited vocabulary.

The first attacker lunged with a knife. Julian sidestepped with liquid grace, catching the man's wrist and using his own momentum to drive the blade into the attacker's thigh. A precise strike—debilitating but not fatal. The man collapsed with a howl.

Two more rushed him simultaneously. Julian dropped to one knee, sweeping the legs from the first while driving his elbow into the second's solar plexus. The impact compressed the diaphragm, forcing air from the man's lungs in an agonized wheeze.

Julian rolled as the fourth attacker's blade sliced through the air where his head had been a heartbeat earlier. Coming up behind the man, he delivered two lightning strikes to pressure points at the base of the skull. The attacker's eyes rolled back, consciousness fleeing before his body hit the floor.

The fifth man was smarter, keeping his distance, a gun appearing in his hand.

Julian didn't hesitate. He grabbed the decorative tea kettle from the table and hurled it. The heavy ceramic struck the gunman's wrist, bones audibly snapping as the weapon clattered to the tatami.

Within fifteen seconds, all five men lay incapacitated. Julian stood calmly, straightening his jacket as if he'd merely paused to adjust his cuffs rather than neutralize five trained fighters.

The silver-haired man behind the table hadn't moved. His expression remained impassive, though a slight lift of his eyebrow suggested something like appreciation.

"Kurosawa-san," Julian said, inclining his head with precise formality. "I believe you have information about my sister."

* * *

The first guard died without registering the presence behind him. The ceramic blade sliced through his throat, blood spraying in a controlled arc that stained the wall but missed the assassin entirely.

They caught the body as it fell, easing it noiselessly to the floor.

The second guard turned at some primal instinct, his hand reaching for his weapon. Too slow. The assassin was already inside his guard, a second blade puncturing upward beneath his sternum, angled to penetrate the heart directly. His mouth opened in silent shock, eyes widening as he recognized his own death in the expressionless mask before him.

They held him upright as life drained from his eyes, then lowered him gently beside his colleague. No wasted motion, no unnecessary force. Death delivered with the economy of true expertise.

The assassin retrieved the security keys from the guard's belt, their gloved fingers never leaving prints. The high-security wing lay beyond the checkpoint, its reinforced door requiring both keycard and code. They studied the keypad briefly, noting the wear patterns on specific digits. Four numbers, used more frequently than others. They tried the most logical combination.

The lock remained red.

They adjusted, trying again with the same four digits in a different sequence. The third attempt succeeded, the door releasing with a soft click that echoed in the empty corridor.

Moving like shadow given form, they navigated the security wing's labyrinthine passages. Two more guards fell—one to a garrote wire that crushed his larynx, another to finger claws that severed the spinal cord at the base of the skull. Each death silent, each body carefully positioned to avoid immediate discovery.

The interrogation room appeared on their right, its reinforced door marked with warnings in Japanese and English. A single officer stood guard, scrolling through his phone with bored indifference.

* * *

Kurosawa smiled thinly, revealing gold-capped incisors that gleamed in the room's subdued lighting. "Are you American?" His English carried a slight accent, each word carefully chosen. "Though I must say, your entrance lacks subtlety."

Julian remained perfectly still, his body relaxed yet poised to explode into violence if necessary. "I'm not here for subtlety. I'm here for information."

"Information," Kurosawa repeated, as if tasting the word. "A valuable commodity. Perhaps more valuable than you realize."

One of the downed guards stirred, reaching for a concealed weapon. Without looking, Julian stomped precisely on the man's wrist, bones cracking under his heel.

The guard subsided with a whimper.

"Don't play coy or I'll take out your gold teeth," Julian continued conversationally, his voice cold. "Mila Varga. Where is she?"

Kurosawa's eyes narrowed slightly. "The marine biologist. Yes, I know of her." He gestured to the cushion across from him. "Perhaps you would sit? Civilized men should discuss such matters properly."

Julian remained standing.

"So I see." Kurosawa sighed, a sound of genuine regret. "I know this name. Mila Varga. I have heard it."

Julian took a step closer, his patience evaporating. "Where is she?"

"Not in my possession," Kurosawa replied, raising a hand in a placating gesture.

Julian moved with blinding speed, seizing Kurosawa by the throat and lifting him bodily from his cushion. The older man made no resistance, his eyes calm despite the lethal pressure on his windpipe.

"Where?" Julian demanded.

"I do not know," Kurosawa rasped. "I swear. I do not know."

* * *

The police officer never saw death approach. One moment he was alone in the corridor, the next a shadow materialized behind him. The assassin's arm snaked around his neck, an application of pressure cutting off blood flow to the brain. The guard's struggles lasted exactly eight seconds before unconsciousness claimed him.

They didn't kill this one—not yet.

Lowering his unconscious form to the floor, they extracted the keys from his belt and approached the interrogation room door.

The small window revealed their target inside —Sofia Costa, still seated at the table, her head bowed as she worked at something in her lap.

The lock yielded to the guard's key. They pushed the door open silently, ceramic blade ready in their right hand.

And then the door jammed.

The assassin frowned, pushing harder.

But the door wouldn't open. Only then, did they realize that one of the chairs was missing from where it should've been opposite Sofia.

They peered through the opening... The chair was jammed under the handle. Crude, yet effective. A blockade.

Only now did Sofia look up. Her cuffs were dangling off one wrist. Her eyes peered through the dark, spotting the figure in the doorway.

She went completely still.

They licked their lips behind their mask.

Sofia hesitated, as if wondering whether she should scream. It wouldn't matter. There was no one left on the third floor to come help even if she had.

They shoved the door more firmly. But the blockade held.

Sofia closed her mouth. She didn't scream, didn't shout. Her eyes narrowed, and slowly, she approached the door.

CHAPTER 15

"Did Valezzi send you?" Sofia asked, standing in the dingy interrogation room.

She faced the inky figure out in the dark hallway. Behind the dark clad smear of shadow, she spotted multiple dead or dying men. Police officers left in pools of their own blood.

Sofia didn't try to shout. Didn't issue threats.

She used her words, her strongest weapons. Inwardly, her heart pounded a mile a minute. This was the same as when she and Julian had faced the shark.

The assassin didn't respond to Sofia's question. Instead, they pushed harder against the door, the chair legs screeching against the floor as they slowly gained ground. Their silence was more terrifying than any threat—this was someone who didn't need words to communicate deadly intent.

Sofia backed away, mind racing. The chair wouldn't hold much longer. The masked figure's gloved fingers curled around the door's edge, applying methodical pressure that bent the metal hinges with each push.

A crack appeared in the chair's wooden back.

Sofia lunged for the second chair, dragging it across the floor with a metallic screech. She upended it, jamming its legs alongside the first blockade, reinforcing the barricade. The assassin paused, assessing the new obstacle, then resumed pushing with renewed force.

Both chairs groaned under the pressure.

Sofia glanced frantically around the room. No windows, no other doors. Just the table, the chairs, and the two-way mirror reflecting her desperate face back at her. Behind that glass lay her only chance—an observation room that might connect to a different corridor.

The assassin made a sound then—a soft curse in a language Sofia couldn't identify. Not Japanese. Not any European tongue she recognized.

Suddenly, the pressure on the door ceased. Through the narrow opening, Sofia watched the black-clad figure turn away, moving with inhuman grace toward one of the fallen guards. The assassin crouched, hands searching methodically through the dead officer's clothing.

For his weapon.

The realization hit Sofia like ice water. Once armed, the assassin wouldn't need to enter—they could simply shoot her through the gap in the door. She'd be trapped, a fish in a barrel.

Sofia grabbed the metal table, adrenaline lending her strength as she flipped it onto its side. She dragged it toward the two-way mirror. Physics had never been her strongest subject, but survival was a powerful teacher.

Using the table's edge as a battering ram, she slammed it against the mirror's lower corner. The glass vibrated but held. She struck again, harder, the impact jarring her bones. A spiderweb of cracks appeared.

Behind her, she heard the distinctive click of a gun's safety being disengaged.

Sofia threw her entire body weight behind the table, driving it into the weakened glass. The mirror shattered with a crystalline explosion, revealing the darkened observation room beyond. Shards rained down as she clambered onto the table, ignoring the cuts on her palms as she pulled herself through the jagged opening.

The first bullet missed her by centimeters,

embedding itself in the wall as she tumbled into the observation room. The second tore through her jacket sleeve, grazing her upper arm. The sharp sting barely registered through her adrenaline.

Sofia landed hard on the floor amidst broken glass, rolling to absorb the impact. The observation room was small, utilitarian—a desk with monitoring equipment, two chairs, and mercifully, a door. She scrambled toward it as a third shot shattered what remained of the mirror.

The assassin was already squeezing through the opening in the interrogation room door.

They followed in a gazelle sprint across the shattered glass, now climbing through the smashed window after her. Sofia burst through the door into an empty hallway, the overhead lights flickering erratically, casting strobing shadows that transformed the corridor into something from a nightmare.

She broke into a dead sprint, bare feet silent against the cold linoleum.

Left at the first intersection, right at the second—moving on pure instinct through the labyrinthine police station. Behind her, she heard nothing—no footsteps, no breathing, just the occasional soft brush of fabric against walls that told her the assassin pursued.

Sofia rounded a corner and nearly collided with a fallen body—another guard, throat slashed. The assassin had been thorough, eliminating everyone in their path to reach her.

She leapt over the corpse, trying not to think about how many others lay cooling in the empty building.

The emergency stairwell appeared ahead. Sofia slammed through the door, taking the steps three at a time, descending into deeper darkness as the backup lighting failed on the lower levels. Her hand skimmed the railing, using it to guide her momentum rather than slow her pace.

Two floors down, she heard the stairwell door above her open with a soft whisper of hydraulics. The assassin was following, their pace unhurried yet somehow keeping pace.

Sofia pushed harder, her lungs burning, feet slapping against concrete steps.

The ground floor door loomed ahead.

Sofia burst into the main lobby—a cavernous space now transformed into a mausoleum. Bodies were arranged around the central desk, positioned as if they had simply fallen asleep at their posts.

Only the expanding pools of crimson beneath them revealed the truth.

Sofia darted behind the reception counter, searching frantically for weapons, keys, anything useful. Her fingers closed around a key fob with the police department logo—a patrol car key. She pocketed it, then moved toward the main entrance, careful to stay low.

The glass doors were locked, secured for the night shift.

Sofia examined the electronic keypad, noting the worn numbers—a simple four-digit code, likely changed monthly. Standard protocol would use the current month and year. She punched in 0822—August 2022.

The lock remained red.

Behind her, the stairwell door opened with that same whisper of well-oiled hinges.

Sofia tried again—2208, reversing the digits. Nothing. She glanced over her shoulder, spotting the assassin's shadow stretching across the lobby floor. They moved with the patient certainty of someone who knew their prey had nowhere to go.

The gun in their hand gleamed dully under the emergency lights.

Sofia's mind raced, considering and discarding options. Then she spotted it—

a small placard beside the door listing emergency procedures. At the bottom, partially obscured by a coffee stain: "Current evacuation code: 7734"

She punched in the numbers, and the lock flashed green.

Sofia shouldered through the door into the humid night air, immediately darting sideways rather than running straight ahead.

The bullet that would have found her spine shattered the glass door instead.

She zigzagged across the parking lot, using parked patrol cars for cover.

The key fob in her hand chirped as she pressed it frantically, seeking its matching vehicle. On the third press, headlights flashed twenty yards to her right—a standard-issue Toyopet patrol car.

Sofia sprinted toward it, hearing rather than seeing the assassin emerge from the building behind her. She reached the car, yanking the door open and throwing herself inside. Her trembling fingers fumbled with the ignition as a bullet shattered the passenger window, showering her with safety glass.

The engine roared to life. Sofia slammed the transmission into reverse, accelerating blindly. Another shot punched through the windshield, missing her by inches. She shifted to drive, tires screaming as she carved a sharp turn toward the exit.

In her rearview mirror, the assassin stood in the middle of the parking lot, gun raised for another shot. Their posture was relaxed, almost casual—a professional taking careful aim.

Sofia jerked the wheel hard left, then right, creating an unpredictable target as she raced toward the security gate. The barrier was down, a solid metal arm blocking her exit. She didn't slow, instead accelerating toward it with grim determination.

The patrol car smashed through the barrier with a satisfying crunch of metal and plastic. Sofia fishtailed onto the main road, the accelerator pressed to the floor as she fled into the neon-lit streets of Naha's entertainment district.

Her heart hammered against her ribs as she navigated the unfamiliar roads, taking random turns to shake any pursuit. After ten minutes of evasive driving, she pulled into an alley behind a bustling night market, cutting the engine and slumping against the steering wheel.

The shallow gash on her arm had begun to throb, blood seeping through her torn sleeve.

Sofia examined it in the dim light—a clean wound, painful but not serious.

More concerning was the realization of what she'd just escaped.

That assassin hadn't been yakuza. Their methods were too refined. This was someone with specialized training—military, perhaps, but with a level of skill that transcended conventional special forces.

And they had come specifically for her.

Sofia closed her eyes briefly, forcing her breathing to slow. She needed to think, to plan. Julian was walking into a yakuza stronghold, unaware that something far more dangerous than organized crime was hunting them.

She checked the patrol car's equipment—a radio, a first aid kit, a roadside emergency kit. No weapons, but the tools would have to do. Sofia bandaged her arm, then studied the city map in the car's navigation system.

The Jade Dragon club was fifteen minutes away. Julian would be there by now, possibly already inside.

Sofia put the car in gear, determination hardening her features. Whatever game Natasha was playing, whatever web they'd stumbled into, one thing was clear—she and Julian needed to find Mila and get out of Japan before that assassin found them again.

CHAPTER 16

The rain had slicked the street into a dark mirror, broken only by the sodium flare of streetlamps and the occasional sweep of headlights.

Sofia sat in the borrowed police car, the wipers beating a nervous rhythm. She tapped the heel of her boot against the floorboard, restless, waiting. Every passing shadow made her shoulders tighten.

The agreed-upon corner was quiet, just the hiss of tires on wet pavement and the distant hum of the port cranes shifting in the storm wind. She checked the clock. Ten minutes past the time Julian had said.

Then movement. A figure broke from the alley, staggering into the weak light. Julian.

Her breath caught.

He was a mess—shirt torn, face drawn tight with exhaustion, his corduroy jacket spattered dark. Not his blood, she realized at once, though plenty of it. He yanked the car door open and collapsed into the passenger seat with a groan.

Sofia stared.

She'd read the text he'd sent to coordinate the meeting again and again. But she couldn't keep the disbelief and disappointment from her voice. "The yakuza leader doesn't have Mila?"

Julian leaned his head back against the seat, blinking at her. His blue eyes were rimmed red, the whites spidered with burst capillaries. He gave one shallow nod. "I'm sure."

The words landed like stones in her stomach. But her own disappointment was nothing compared to his.

"You're bleeding," she said automatically, her gaze tracking the crimson streaks across his knuckles.

"Not mine." He gave a humorless chuckle, half cough, half laugh.

She wanted to scold him, to demand why he always walked into hellfire alone. Instead, she felt her throat tighten. "Julian…"

He turned his head slowly toward her. "What?"

"I wasn't safe, either."

His expression sharpened. "What

happened?"

Sofia gripped the steering wheel. The leather was slick beneath her palms, her knuckles whitening. "There was an attack. At the station." She drew in a breath, slow, unsteady. "One man. He came out of nowhere. Moved like—like a phantom. Like a... I know how it sounds but like a ninja, Julian. I've never seen anything like it."

Julian sat up straighter, the exhaustion burning away in an instant. "He got to you? Inside a police station?"

She nodded, her jaw trembling despite herself. "He killed officers. So many. I thought—" She broke off, shutting her eyes briefly. "I thought I was next."

A beat of silence. Then Julian slammed his palm against the dash. The sound cracked through the car like a gunshot, and when he pulled his hand away, a bloody handprint smeared across the plastic.

"Who sent him?" His voice was low, guttural, dangerous.

"I don't know." Her answer was barely above a whisper. A shiver went through her whole body at the memory.

Julian reached across, careful not to smear her with his bloodied hand, and wrapped his arm around her shoulders in a quick, protective squeeze. It wasn't long, but it steadied her in a way words couldn't. Then he pulled back, jaw set like stone.

"Tell me everything."

She did. The terse, clipped details of her escape. The way she'd slipped through chaos while the assassin carved his way deeper into the station. The certainty in her bones that this was no ordinary hitman.

Julian listened, face darkening with each word.

When she finished, he exhaled hard. "All right. We're not staying here." He jabbed a finger at the windshield. "Drive."

She shifted the car into gear, and they rolled forward into the empty street.

The silence of the hour was broken suddenly by a wail—long, sonorous, mechanical. Sirens.

Not police sirens. Bigger. Broader.

Town sirens.

Both of them froze for an instant. Then Julian twisted the dial on the radio, static crackling through the speakers until a clear voice broke through, urgent and rapid.

Sofia leaned closer, translating under her

breath. "Another typhoon. Stronger than the first. Making landfall within hours."

Julian gave a humorless laugh. "Perfect. Because this wasn't complicated enough already."

She didn't smile. "Where is Mila, Julian? She told you she'd stay put. But she didn't. Which means she was hiding something—from you, from everyone."

His jaw flexed. "She promised."

"She was deceiving someone." Sofia's voice sharpened, her gaze flicking toward him. "What if... what if she knew someone was reading her messages? Someone was listening in."

"Might explain why she misled me. For the sake of misleading *them.* But who? Who would have that sort of access?"

Sofia considered this. She frowned. "Maybe law enforcement. Maybe a research partner. Someone who might've been intercepting her calls or texts."

Julian swore softly, rubbing at his temple.

He dug his phone out and dialed.

"Hiro," he barked when the line connected. "Get Emi. And anyone else close to Mila. No... no this is offical. You have to come." A pause. "That's right, or I'll arrest every damn one of you."

Sofia winced. But it seemed, by Julian's slowly relaxing posture, that his bluff worked. For now.

"I'm texting you the address of a police shelter. Tell them to come. As in *right now.*"

He hung up and rubbed at his eyes.

"A, er, police shelter?" Sofia asked. "Is that a thing?"

"Interpol safehouse." Julian's voice softened only slightly. "Old one. Secure. We'll hole up there and get answers without uniforms breathing down our necks. Here—my phone. That's the address."

The wipers slapped faster as the rain thickened, the street narrowing into a funnel of neon and shadow. Sofia drove in silence, watching his reflection in the windshield. He looked like hell—bloodied, battered, but unbroken. His eyes caught briefly in the glow of a passing sign, fierce even through fatigue.

They reached the safehouse on the edge of town—an unremarkable concrete block disguised as a municipal archive building. Julian punched in a code on the door's keypad, and the heavy lock disengaged with a thunk.

Inside, the space was utilitarian: steel tables, fluorescent lights, a bank of dusty filing cabinets. A generator hummed faintly somewhere below, the air smelling of disinfectant and old paper.

Julian paced, restless, like a wolf in too small a cage. "It'll have to. We don't have anywhere else."

About an hour later, the first figures arrived—wet coats, anxious faces. Hiro. Emi. The researcher had pulled his ponytail back with an elastic band. The student's blue-tipped hair was wet and dripping in her wide eyes. The door banged shut against the wind and Emi blurted, "Is Mila-sensei okay? You found her?"

Julian's smile didn't reach his eyes. "That's why we're here."

Four more bodies pressed in behind Hiro and Emi, pushed by the gale. They shook off water and nerves in equal measure. Hiro cleared his throat, glasses fogging again, and lifted a hand as if he were taking attendance.

"I told them it was under Interpol authority," he said, tone apologetic but firm. "This is Dr. Reiko Tanaka—operations. She keeps us from drowning on land."

Reiko dipped a precise nod, navy raincoat beaded with rain, a folder clutched to her chest as if even paper needed shelter. "We're here to cooperate," she said, English careful and clipped. Her eyes slid to the blood on Julian's cuffs and flinched back, as though politeness could erase what she'd seen.

"And Kenji Morita," Hiro continued, "our dive master—"

Kenji cut in, voice gravel rough. "I can say my own name," he said, stepping forward with the square solidity of a man who trusts decks more than floors. "Kenji. I run dives, I run safety. If this is really Interpol, I want a lawyer before we 'cooperate' our way into trouble." He folded his arms and stared at Julian as if he were sizing up a rip current. "No offense."

"Plenty taken," Julian said pleasantly, already reaching for the kettle. "But let's try tea before litigation."

Emi slid sideways to make space for a tall young woman with a notebook hugged to her chest. "And this is Yumi Sato," she offered quickly, her blue-tipped hair flicking rain. "Master's program. She's been with Mila-sensei on the youth outreach dives."

Yumi's smile tried to exist and failed. "I—hello." Whale stickers crowded the spine of her notebook; her thumbs pressed the edges white.

Hiro's hand hovered to the last arrival. "Tomasz Kowalski bioacoustics. He records the pods. Humpbacks like him more than they like the rest of us."

Tomasz gave a tight nod, the small case slung over his shoulder like a reliquary. "They like no one," he muttered in a Polish-rough baritone. "We just listen better some days."

"And I'm Reiko, again," Reiko added, as if tidiness demanded symmetry. "If there are forms, I'll fill them."

"Phones and wallets on the tray, please," Sofia said, Japanese first, then English. "Storm protocol—keep valuables dry and together so they don't go missing in the shuffle. You'll get everything back when we're done."

A hesitation went through the room, a soft, collective hitch. The word *Interpol* had rearranged the air.

Then, one by one, they obeyed: Reiko first, placing a neat black wallet; Kenji setting down a battered flip phone with a faint clang; Yumi adding a pink-cased smartphone face down, student pass flashing under the rubber; Tomasz reluctantly parting with his own, but keeping a hand on the strap of his recorder as if to say *this one is different*; Emi's clear case with a tiny whale charm; and finally Hiro, the matte-black rectangle.

Julian moved among them with a host's easy patter, laying out paper cups, pouring tea that smelled vaguely of cardboard. "Thank you for trudging through a storm for a meeting no one wants. Consider this a sleepover with terrible beverages and better answers."

Kenji snorted. "I'll take the answers."

"You and me both," Julian said, the corners of his eyes crinkling, worry hidden and not. "We're here because Mila matters. If you truly don't know anything, say so. If you do—this is the room to speak before the power goes and the coastguard turns this island into a locked box."

Emi's fingers tightened around her cup. "Mila-sensei wouldn't want secrets."

Sofia watched the way she said it—chin up, defiance propping fear. She had a small heart drawn on her wrist with marker which she kept itching at.

Sofia drifted back to the tray, hands efficient, gentle. She kept her back to the group so they couldn't quite see what she was doing. She placed each phone and wallet on a clean towel, turning them as if she were merely keeping track, not reading the lives pressed flat inside. A ferry ticket tucked in Reiko's bills—last Thursday to Naha. A cracked hinge on Kenji's phone that had weathered a thousand panicked opens. A spectrogram printout folded in Tomasz's wallet where a photo might have lived. Yumi's ATM slip from two days ago. Emi's lock screen: Mila, laughing over a tide pool with children. Hiro's privacy filter catching the light at just the right angle to make the screen unreadable from anywhere but straight on.

Outside, the sirens deepened again. The shutters rattled. The kettle clicked off. Julian set it back on its base and leaned a hip against the table like a man about to deal cards.

"All right," he said softly. "Let's talk about Mila."

"It's just a conversation," Sofia added, almost cheerful, almost true. "No interrogation. But we're going to be very, very honest with one another."

She glanced once at Julian. He gave her the smallest nod.

Then, as Sofia turned back to the tray, one of the phones lit up and buzzed—silent, insistent. A name flashed across the screen, and her breath caught.

The storm roared approval. The power flickered.

Kenji's phone.

On the tiny external screen: **KOVIĆ, NATASHA**.

CHAPTER 16

Sofia caught Julian's eye, nodding towards the tray. He frowned and drew near. Looked down.

She glanced over at Kenji. He didn't seem to notice and was busy staring into his cup of tea.

Sofia's gaze snapped back to Julian. He didn't ask permission. He rarely did. He flipped the phone open and stabbed the green button.

"Why does he have your number?" Julian said by way of greeting. No hello, no preamble. "Why does a local dive master have *Natasha Ković* saved in his phone?"

A beat of bandwidth hush, then Natasha's voice, crisp and cool through storms of static. "Julian. Good. You're in one piece. Bring Costa in. Now. I want to know what happened at the police station."

Julian's laugh was a knife that didn't bother being sheathed. "Bite me, Ković. Why is your name in *his* phone—and why does *he* have it saved?"

"Come in," she repeated, colder. "Costa is wanted for questioning—"

"Wanted for bullshit, you mean." He turned away from the others, voice dropping. "Answer the question."

Silence stretched just long enough to be its own message. The storm pressed against the shutters, a palm trying to flatten the building.

"Come in," Natasha said again. "This place is a killing field. What the hell happened? What did Sofia do?"

Julain hung up. He closed the phone softly, then wheeled on Kenji.

The dive instructor now seemed to have realized his phone was the source of consternation. He stared at them. Expressionless.

Julian wasted no time. He pointed an accusing finger. "Tell me what you know. Right *now*."

Kenji's jaw worked. The brashness he'd worn at the door splintered, leaving something older—seaworn stubbornness, yes, but also a flicker of fear. "I don't know," he said. "I don't—"

Sofia stepped between them before Julian's temper finished the job. She turned to face Kenji, gentling her tone like lowering a sail. "You said you run dives and safety. I believe you." Her voice warmed a degree. "You also care about Mila. Don't you?"

Kenji didn't answer. He looked at the floor.

Sofia waited. The silence was not empty; it was invitation. She watched the tiny tells—how his shoulders rose on the inhale and failed to fall all the way on the exhale; how his gaze kept drifting toward Hiro and then away, as if an answer might be hiding in the smaller man's posture. She softened her stance, uncrossed everything that could be uncrossed, became a person you could tell a secret to.

"Someone asked you to keep an eye on her," she said, not a question, just a step placed exactly where his weight already leaned.

A muscle jumped in Kenji's cheek. "To… make sure she was all right. Nothing illegal." His voice roughened. "Said she had trouble with…attention she didn't want."

"Who asked?" Julian said.

Kenji swallowed. "A European woman. Police, I thought. She had that look." He risked a glance at the phone on the towel. "She gave me a number to call if anything seemed wrong. It came with…compensation. Not much." He lifted one shoulder, ashamed. "I thought I was helping."

"Did you call her?" Sofia asked.

Kenji hesitated—too long for a man deciding whether to lie. "Twice. Once when the first storm warning hit and Mila didn't come in with the others. And once three days ago."

"What changed three days ago?" Julian's voice was calm now, which was always more dangerous.

Kenji wet his lips. He stared at the tea in his cup as if the steam could spell it out for him. "She began acting...strange. Not scared. Suspicious. She asked me, in this casual way that wasn't casual, if anyone at the station could look up phone records."

Reiko's head lifted. "Phone records?"

"Not ours," Kenji said quickly. "Like...is it possible to see who called who. Logs. She said it like a joke." His eyes flicked to Hiro, then away. "I told her I didn't know."

"Does anyone?" Sofia asked the room, turning a fraction so her question fell on more than one pair of ears. "Access to lab call logs, router history, anything that would tell us who's calling whom?"

Reiko cleared her throat. "Internal calls? Yes. The VoIP system is logged. But that's internal extensions, not personal mobiles." She looked at Hiro. "Server credentials are IT's and mine. And Daichi's."

"Where's Daichi?" Julian asked.

"At his home," Reiko said, frustration tightening the words. "He left the day before the first storm. Ferry shut down after."

The generator hiccupped; the lights browned and recovered.

Sofia turned back to Kenji. "What else changed?"

He held her gaze and then surrendered to it. "She stopped letting anyone else pack the boat." The admission came out in a rush. "Usually, she makes a joke, lets students help. But three days ago, before she left for Kagami-shima, she loaded everything herself. Told Yumi to go home and sleep." His mouth tightened. "And she told me not to worry. Mila never says that unless there is something to worry about."

Yumi flinched. "She said it kindly," she murmured. "Not like a dismissal."

Sofia nodded, absorbing it. "Kenji, when you called Natasha three days ago, what did you report?"

"That she had taken the small research boat alone. That she told the girl not to follow."

He glanced at Emi; the girl looked down at her hands.

"What did the woman say?" Julian asked.

Kenji's mouth opened, closed. "Just…'good.' And 'call if she returns early.' I had the feeling that they were going to redirect her to somewhere safer."

He looked ashamed. "I thought it was routine. I thought it meant protection. You know—police shadowing, not…whatever this is."

Sofia let the softness drain from her tone by a degree. "Natasha is not local police. She's Interpol. If she put you on her string, Kenji, she should have told us—and she didn't."

Kenji winced at *string*. "I didn't know she was…" He gestured, broad, encompassing whatever Interpol meant to him. "She never said. She didn't give a name at first. Later, I saved the number as she told me: Ković. I thought it made it official." The last word came out small.

The wind hit the shutters with a hollow boom. Somewhere in the hills, another siren started—lower, closer.

"Three days ago," Sofia repeated, "Did anyone else notice changes?"

Emi glanced at Hiro, and he, at the floor.

Finally, Hiro said, "She stopped eating dinner with us. She stayed in the archive until early morning two nights in a row." He pushed his glasses up, lenses smeared by the gesture. "When I asked, she said she was 'creating some space.'" His mouth twisted.

Tomasz shifted his weight. "She borrowed an extra hydrophone," he said, reluctant, as if saying it might make it matter more than it had. "Did not log it. I found the drawer open."

"For whales?" Julian asked.

Tomasz shook his head. "Maybe. But you do not need two for the pods she studies —unless you are triangulating something. Or someone."

Sofia's pulse caught and then smoothed. "Or recording a call made from underwater." She said it lightly, as if trying it on to see if it fit, but the room felt it land.

Reiko hugged her folder tighter. "We are scientists," she said, almost pleading. "This is starting to sound like—"

"Like what it is," Julian said. "A hunt."

The generator coughed again; the lights dimmed to a smoky yellow. Rain came harder, a fist loosening only to swing back again.

Sofia returned to Kenji, softening once more. "When Natasha texted or called you—

what name did she use for Mila?"

Kenji frowned, surprised. "She didn't. She didn't use names. She wrote 'the subject.'" His discomfort deepened. "I didn't like it."

"Did she ever ask you to do anything besides watch?" Sofia asked, almost conversational, as if they were discussing tide charts.

Kenji's eyes cut sideways. That was the tell; that was the crack.

"She asked me to check the guesthouse lights at odd hours," he confessed. "Twice. To see if anyone had returned. She said if I saw lights on late, I should call her and not go in." He swallowed. "I didn't ask why."

Julian leaned on the table, palms flat, bleeding patience. "And did you?"

"One night before the first storm," Kenji said. "Lights on, very late. I called. The lights went out ten minutes later."

"Did you see who left?" Sofia asked.

"No." He shook his head. "The rain—visibility was bad."

Sofia let silence rest again; she felt the room rearrange around it. She could almost hear her mentor's voice—*Ask the right question once. Then let the answer take up space it needs.*

"Kenji," she said quietly, "why didn't you tell us this at the start?"

He stared at his hands. "Because I thought it would make me the enemy," he said. "And I am not. I would take a broken rib for that girl." He lifted his chin, grief and pride in the act. "Most of us here would."

Emi nodded, fierce, as if to slam the statement into the floor like a nail.

Sofia believed him. It didn't make anything simpler.

She pivoted. "Reiko—the VoIP logs. Where are they housed?"

"On the local server," Reiko said. "Mirrored to the mainland weekly—when ferries run."

"And now?" Julian asked.

"Now the ferry is closed," she said. "And the island's uplink is throttled by the storm. Even if I could connect, power will be intermittent. You saw the lights."

"Local access?" Sofia pressed.

Reiko's mouth thinned. "At the station, on my terminal. And Daichi's."

Hiro scrubbed at his jaw. "If power holds for thirty minutes, I could try a remote pull," he said, not meeting anyone's eyes. "No promises. The router's been sulking since the last surge."

The building creaked as a gust shouldered it. The lights guttered, caught, steadied. The sirens bellowed a fresh round, lower, more insistent, as if the island were being told to go to ground and stay there.

Julian blew out a breath and leaned back, the fight in him re-leashing itself by an inch. "So: we have a shadow babysitter set by Interpol, a wreck Mila couldn't stop visiting, and a lab that might be logging calls we can't reach." He glanced at Sofia, humor surfacing only as armor. "Progress."

Sofia didn't answer. She watched the people in front of her.

"Fine," she said at last, voice calm, the calm that announces the opposite. "We split the problems. Hiro, try the remote pull. Reiko, write down every internal extension Mila used in the last month—anyone she called more than once. Tomasz, list what equipment went missing or was borrowed without log signatures, starting two weeks ago." She turned to Kenji. "You and I will map times you drove by the guesthouse and when you called Natasha."

Kenji nodded, relief and dread braided together.

"And me?" Yumi asked, small, steady.

Sofia looked at her. "You tell me the last time you heard Mila truly laugh," she said. "And what came right before that."

Yumi blinked, startled. Then, softly: "When she showed the children how to hear shrimp snapping through a pipe. The day before she stopped eating with us." Her throat bobbed. "Before the woman came."

Sofia felt that settle in her chest.

The generator thumped. The lights dimmed and didn't quite return to full. The room grew narrower, the air thicker, the storm's voice fuller, closer, as if it had found a door left ajar and put its mouth to it.

Julian checked Kenji's phone again, thumbed to the call log, glanced at the timestamp, then set it down like evidence that wouldn't yet testify. He met Sofia's eyes across the table—there was an entire conversation there, unfinished.

"Feels like a dead end," he said lightly.

"It will until it doesn't," Sofia said. She almost smiled. "That's the job."

The sirens wailed anew. Somewhere outside, a transformer cracked like a tree being torn in half.

No one moved for a long breath. The storm had the room by the throat.

"Okay," Julian said at last, the word an exhale and a promise. "We keep going."

They did. But the typhoon pressed closer, the walls listening, the island flattening its breath—and for the first time since they'd stepped into the safehouse, it felt like Mila was further away, not nearer.

CHAPTER 17

The safehouse had an after-midnight hush, the kind that makes machines sound like animals. The generator purred under the floor. Pipes clicked. Wind worried the shutters. In the main room, a scatter of borrowed blankets rose and fell with the sleep of people who had run out of adrenaline and choices.

Julian didn't sleep.

He stood at the folding table under the flickering strip light, elbow-deep in a cardboard banker's box Reiko had insisted on carrying "just in case." Inventory lists, staff notices, a paper directory someone had printed last month and stapled crooked. His fingers, still stained at the knuckles, turned pages with a gentleness that didn't match his eyes.

"Found something," he murmured when Sofia brushed past, refilling the kettle with bottled water. She didn't ask what, not yet. He was in the particular stillness he got when anger had finally conceded the wheel to concentration.

He tapped a sheet he'd pulled from the bottom of the stack—**Call Server Access Log – Weekly Summary**. The print was faint, dot-matrix pale, but the times jumped anyway: log-ins around midnight, again at 04:10, again at noon. Always the same admin account. Always the same workstation ID.

"Daichi," Sofia said softly. Hiro had mentioned him earlier. Systems. On the mainland, allegedly.

Julian's jaw moved. "Everyone swears he took a ferry before the storm. But this workstation ID is assigned to the server annex at the station. If he's been logging in this often, someone's at his desk."

"Or tunneling," Sofia said. "VPN, spoofing." She didn't sound convinced. Storms throttle uplinks; islands close like fists. "Either way, it's not nothing."

Julian had a second sheet beneath the first. **Emergency Contact & Residence File**.

"Address," he said simply, tapping where someone had written in neat black ink: **Nakamura, Daichi — Minami Ridge, Building 3, Unit 402.** A penciled arrow pointed up from the note: **Key with landlord.** Below it, a landline number with a local exchange.

Sofia set the kettle down without turning it on. "We wait until morning," she said, because that was the right answer.

"No," Julian said, because he couldn't.

The storm thudded its argument into the shutters, a heavy palm.

"Julian. We have six people sleeping who trust us to keep them from being stupid tonight. There's a typhoon trying to climb in through the roof. The roads will be—"

"Closed," he finished. The word tasted like rules. "And in the morning, if he's part of this, he'll have had eight more hours to wash it clean."

She looked at him for a long breath. He was pale with exhaustion, eyes raw, mouth cut into a line that promised he would not forgive himself for anything that looked like waiting. She wanted to press the logic into him like a bandage. She wanted to give him what she could.

"Natasha has satellite," he said suddenly, as if remembering a tool in the bottom of a drawer. "Live traffic overlays. Weather models. She can thread us through it."

Sofia's head tilted. "She will also thread a net around me the second we come into range."

"I'll call her." He was already picking up Kenji's battered phone, thumb smearing its cracked plastic clean. The name **KOVIĆ, NATASHA** glowed like a dare. "I'll tell her I'm bringing you in. I'll ask for road status and safe corridors. We'll use them, and then—" He shrugged. "We won't go where she expects."

It was reckless. It was effective. It was him.

Sofia let out a breath she hadn't realized she'd been holding. "Five minutes," she said. "To pack. Then we tell Kenji and Emi we're leaving. Everyone else stays put. If the roof comes off, the food's in the back cupboard, top shelf—rice, canned fish, stove fuel."

Julian looked up, gratitude moving through his tired face like a tide. "Thank you."

"Don't thank me yet," she said, and went to gather an emergency kit.

She took the satellite phone Hiro had given them earlier, a small first-aid case, two mylar blankets, a waterproof flashlight, the slim prybar she liked better than a gun in close quarters, a roll of tape. She slid her little yellow pencil into her bun without thinking and then immediately took it out and hooked it to her belt loop.

Kenji stirred when she touched his shoulder. He woke fast, a diver's reflex, eyes already on the door.

"We're going out," Sofia whispered, kneeling so her voice wouldn't carry. "Stay here. Lock the door after us. If the power dies, the generator switch is marked with tape. Food's in back—top shelf."

Kenji frowned. "In this?"

"In this," Julian answered from the doorway. "If we're not back by dawn, you keep everyone here until midday. No heroics."

Emi sat up, hair sticking up in salt-soft spikes. "Where are you going?"

"Minami Ridge," Sofia said. "Daichi's place."

Emi's mouth formed a perfect O. "But the roads—"

"We know," Julian said, already moving. "Don't let anyone leave. Not for anything."

They stepped into the hallway. The safehouse door moaned against the pressure differential when they pulled it open, and then the typhoon punched them full in the face.

Rain like nails. Wind like a wall.

The borrowed police car crouched black and low under pines that thrashed their disbelief. Julian hunched into the gale and half ran for the driver's side, cupping a hand to shield the phone as he dialed. Sofia slid into the passenger seat and slammed the door; the sound was swallowed instantly by the roar outside. The car smelled of wet vinyl and the ghost of cigarettes.

He put the call on speaker.

"Ković," Natasha said, voice crisp, as if she were warm and dry.

"It's me," Julian said. He sounded casual and didn't look it. "Bringing Costa in. Need corridors. Which roads aren't lakes and which bridges still exist."

A pause. The polite scrape of a chair in a different world. "I'm sending you a secure link. Sat overlay plus prefectural advisories. Stay on highlighted corridors. Do not deviate."

"I love it when you talk to me like a fire marshal," he said, and there was the ghost of his old grin. "Thanks."

"Julian," Natasha added, clean as a scalpel, "if you do not bring Costa straight to the station, I will issue a BOLO that will make this island feel smaller than it already is."

"Understood," he lied, and cut the call.

Sofia arched an eyebrow. "We are going to hell."

"Wind at our backs," he said, and showed her the map blooming on his screen: arteries of yellow through a city gone blue with flood. He traced a finger from their pin to Minami

Ridge. "An hour if the gods are napping."

"They're not."

He put the car in gear.

They slid down the hill in first, tires whispering over pine needles and water. The sirens were a constant now, not a warning but a condition of air.

Streetlights bowed to the wind. Somewhere behind them, metal clanged—a sign folding in on itself.

Sofia watched the way the rain moved, learning its speed, its angles. Language had taught her that tone was content in disguise; storms were the same. This one spoke in two registers: a low, endless moan; a high, brittle hiss.

The radio burbled in Japanese: bridge closures, landslide advisories, evacuation centers. She translated automatically, then caught herself. "You don't need—"

"I like the sound," Julian said. "It makes this feel like a solvable equation."

They passed the harbor. The water had climbed the steps and was pawing at the market stalls, foam licking at the tarps. A fishing boat lay half on its side on the street like a creature sleeping in the wrong place. The air smelled thick with iodine and snapped pine.

"Turn back if it gets stupid," Sofia said. She meant it. She'd say it again.

He didn't answer. He leaned forward over the wheel the way he did when he was about to pick a lock, eyes narrow, mouth soft and stubborn. He blinked when he thought. He was blinking a lot.

The first obstacle was a tree. An old one, trunk split like a broken tooth, draped across the road, branches clawing at the asphalt. Julian eased the car to a stop. Rain hammered the windshield so hard it looked like metal.

"We can go around," he said, seeing something she didn't yet. He backed up, cut into a narrow lane glistening like a cellar floor, threaded between two houses so close she could see pictures on a wall through a window: a wedding, a school uniform, someone's grandfather with a fish he'd been proud of. The car's antenna scraped a string of windbells.

Back on the main road, the map told him to follow the coastal curve. He didn't. "That'll be under," he said, and cut inland. The tires found water and lost it and found it again. At one point a sheet of corrugated tin shot past them in the beam of the headlights like a playing card thrown by an angry god.

They hit an open stretch where the wind

had room to run. The car shuddered. Sofia pressed a hand to the dash without knowing why, as if to keep the engine in its seat. "This is —"

"Stupid," he said, but his hands were steady.

They climbed. The town fell away into a tangle of black streets laced white with runoff. Farther up, power was out. Houses hunched like animals with their eyes closed. A shrine's red gate leaned sideways at an angle that made her teeth ache.

"Look," he said suddenly, and pointed with his chin. On the ridge ahead, through the rain, a dim rectangle of light. "Minami."

The road narrowed to a ribbon that flirted with the edge of air. The cliff on their right had shed pieces of itself; mud and stones slithered under their tires in little avalanches that wanted to be big ones. Twice, headlights caught the shine of water across the road where a ditch had gone looking for a new home. Twice, he feathered them through.

"Turn back," she said quietly. "We can't rescue anyone if we're upside down in a ravine."

He smiled without joy.

"Julian."

"I hear you."

He did not turn back.

Her watch ticked against her wrist in its small, practical way. Bezopasnost, she told herself without thinking; seguridad; ān quán. She breathed the syllables into her chest.

The thing that saved them wasn't luck. It was the way her eyes habitually dragged the bottom edge of the world.

"Branch!" she shouted, the same instant the headlights lifted a slick, dark limb out of blackness, lying across both lanes like something that had been thrown. Julian jerked the wheel left, then right—two clean cuts—and the car skated sideways, tires hissing, then snapped back into line so hard her teeth clicked.

They came to a stop with the nose angled toward the ditch, both of them breathing like they'd run stairs.

"Okay," he said hoarsely, hands still locked on the wheel. "We're going to—"

The rear window blew out.

CHAPTER 18

The rear window didn't shatter so much as un-exist, glass becoming air and then pellets that rattled across the seats and into their hair. The sound came delayed, a hard, dry **crack** that a different night would have called a gunshot, but tonight could have been the sky itself tearing.

Sofia didn't think. She translated the pattern: the bloom of tempered glass. The line of wind that suddenly had a path into the car.

"Down!" she shouted. "Julian—shots—"

The passenger-side mirror exploded like a flower punched from behind. A second hard crack. A panicked waltz of silver glitter along the road.

Julian's arm was already across her, a force that didn't ask, driving her down so her shoulder hit the transmission tunnel and the glovebox corner jabbed her ribs. He pivoted, twisted, body between hers and the back window, one hand still on the wheel, the other pushing her head down until her face was full of floor mat.

A headrest burst just above her ear. Foam and fabric puffed into the air like dandelion.

"Stay down," he said, voice bent into a shape she had never heard from him. The car lurched forward as he stomped the accelerator.

Two more cracks stuttered off the cliffside; something pinged the roof and went whining into the night.

She could see the pedals, his boots, the hop of his knee as he feathered gas to grip. Rain roared through the new hole in the world. The car fishtailed, corrected, fishtailed again. Wet glass and hot fear was suddenly everything.

"Where?" he demanded, not looking, the question aimed at the storm.

"Up and right. High ground. Tight grouping. Suppressed—storm's masking the report." The words were a ladder; she climbed them out of panic one rung at a time. "They're shooting to disable, not kill. So far."

"So far isn't a plan," he said through his teeth.

"Left turn in twenty meters. Blind curve. If they're smart, they'll try to funnel us into a choke."

"They're smart," he said, and threw the wheel left anyway.

The car took the turn like a dropped plate, skidding, catching, skidding. Another crack, lower this time, an attempt at the tire that he destroyed with motion. They hit a stretch of road where wind did a different thing, a brief slackening like a breath caught between sobs.

"Out of sight," she said. "For five seconds."

"Five seconds is a lifetime," he answered, and killed the headlights.

They plunged into a black so thick it had texture. The rain became a cold curtain; the engine a living thing; the road a rumor. He kept the car moving, slow, silent, coasting the shoulder until the tires found a lip of gravel that felt like safety and maybe was. He cut the engine.

They lay there in the dark, breathing, while the storm moved around them and, somewhere behind, the shooter recalculated a problem that refused to hold still.

"Okay," Julian whispered, so low she felt it more than heard it. "We do not panic. We do not die. We find Daichi."

Sofia's hand found his in the dark. She squeezed once.

Around them, the typhoon raged like a goliath had lost something important in the trees and meant to tear the island apart until it found it. Somewhere up the road, a light stuttered and vanished. Somewhere downhill, water found a new direction and took it.

Another crack. Farther now. Testing.

Julian leaned toward her, breath warm against her ear. "On three," he murmured. "We slide out my side, low. We use the ditch for cover."

She nodded.

"Three," he said.

They moved.

CHAPTER 19

They crawled the ditch like ghosts, hands and knees, breath and rain. The car crouched behind them, a black animal without eyes. Wind took the world by the shoulders and shook.

"Listen," Sofia whispered.

They froze. The storm spoke in two tongues again—low moan, brittle hiss—but beneath it, something else: a patience. Not a sound so much as the absence of one in a shape that meant *watcher*.

Julian leaned close. "He followed us," he breathed into her ear.

"Same signature as the station," she said. "Trained. One pair of feet."

They moved, keeping the cliff to their left where a thatch of shrubs made a hedge against the sky. The lane narrowed to a shelf of black rock. Water sheeted off the ridge in white veils; their clothes stuck to their skin like they'd grown there. Somewhere below, the ocean hit the cliff in a rhythm old as anger.

A stone clinked and danced behind them. Nothing in the storm should have sounded that clean.

Julian's hand closed on her wrist. He tugged her into the shelter of a toppled boulder, breath tight. "We need to flip the board," he murmured. "He has range. We need to take it away."

Sofia swallowed rain. "How?"

He checked the handgun at his waist—wet but fed. "We try a feint," he said. "Draw him to a place he likes, then make him hate it."

"Try and then fail and then almost die? You have a type."

"Work with me."

They bolted from cover to cover—three heartbeats, five, crouch, slide, stand. The path ahead cut inward under an overhang, a wet black mouth just big enough to hide a man inside. It was the kind of geometry a hunter would love.

They darted for it.

He was already there.

A shadow peeled from the rock and moved through the rain like it had learned to speak water. Close enough to smell the oil he kept off his steel. Close enough to see the tongue of scar tissue on the thumb that marks a man who reloads under stress. He drove a heel kick at Julian's knee. Julian caught the impact on his shin, pivoted, answered with an elbow like a door slamming into a face. The shadow folded, flowed, came up with a knife that had never learned the word *rust*.

Sofia lunged to flank him, but a palm like a hammer found her sternum and placed her into the rock. Stars burst. Rain hissed.

Julian went at him then—shoulder, hip, weight. The fight turned slippery and immediate, a grammar of leverage and pain.

The blade nicked fabric, skin.

The gun barked once, close enough that the muzzle flash was a white square inside the storm, but the shot went to noise because the shadow had already moved.

They broke apart, breathing hard. Three beats of distance between them. Rain wrote disappearing cursive between their eyes.

The shadow laughed once, low. He sounded amused at physics.

Julian snapped two quick shots—warning, probing. Lightning stitched the sky and for a strobe-bright instant the assassin was there, edged in white, a cutout against the overhang. Then he wasn't. The rounds pinged somewhere useless, and the shadow slid backward into the stone.

"Cover," Julian hissed.

They fell back ten paces to a collapsed tongue of basalt jutting from the slope. They dropped into the pocket, soaked breath fogging the little space, shoulders pressed to cold rock.

Julian checked his magazine by feel.

Lightning again—empty path, veils of rain, no silhouette. The storm filled every space with noise until noise meant nothing. Sofia listened for what wasn't there: no loose stone kicked, no fabric rasp, no human breath out of rhythm with the hurricane.

"He melted," Julian said softly. "Waiting us out."

"For what?"

"For the second we believe he's gone."

They waited anyway. Ten slow breaths. Fifteen. The typhoon howled. Nothing moved but water.

Julian's eyes found hers in the dark. Calm. Bright. Decided.

"We can't win straight," he said, voice calm, eyes bright.

He pressed the handgun into her palm. The metal felt like a live thing. "Sixty seconds," he said. "Fire anywhere. Just be loud."

"Where are you going?"

"Down," he said, and was gone, a dark shape smearing into the heavier dark of the cliff's edge.

She slid behind a knee-high rock, cliff yawning at her side like an open mouth. She could feel the ocean's climb in her bones. The storm had fingers; it learned faces.

She counted in her head—**one**—and made herself breathe. **Two. Three. Four.** The trick with fear was to give it numbers.

The path lay slick and black and empty. No sign of the hunter. No sign of Julian.

Twenty-six. Twenty-seven. The wind rose and shoved against the rock like a giant had just found them. **Thirty-eight.** The rain changed angle, a signal of nothing but it made her want to stand. **Forty-nine. Fif—**

The gunshot cracked the night apart.

She fired into the sky, into the storm, into the ear of whatever listened. The sound tore free and went running down the ridge.

At the edge of her vision, something moved on the cliff—the shape of a body flowing *up* where bodies don't go. It was wrong and beautiful: hands and feet finding a soaked shelf, weight riding slick basalt with the confidence of a spider. The figure crested the lip as if born from stone and stood, rain sluicing off black cloth.

Sofia turned the gun toward him, but he was already moving.

A flick of the arm, a seam of silver through the storm—the knife. Pain lit her hand as it struck, spinning the pistol from her grip like a toy. The blade's kiss opened her palm; heat bloomed and the rain tried to wash it away.

She stumbled back, heel skidding on algae-slick rock.

The cliff reminded her it did not care, not about physics, not about names. She pinwheeled once, found the rock with her hip. The shadow was on her in two strides. He held a small device in his left hand; its tiny speaker crackled a smooth robotic voice.

"Valezzi sends her regards," the device whispered, polite under apocalypse.

The gun in his right hand rose, steady. It looked like an answer to a question she wasn't finished asking.

Sofia's mind did the only thing it knew how to do in an unwinnable second: it looked for language. *Bezopasnost. Seguridad. Ān quán.* She saw not his gun but his feet, not his face but the tension in his forearm, the minimalism of a man for whom recoil was a memory. No flourish. Just ending.

Then the world hit him sideways.

Julian arrived like a wave that had learned to walk. A low tackle out of the dark, shoulder cutting the man's knees, momentum jamming the pistol high and wide so its shot went shrieking into rain.

They went down hard—two men and a storm—rolling, slamming, tearing at purchase that never existed.

The assassin was fast. He arched, found space that water didn't own, snapped a heel at Julian's ribs. Julian took it on a forearm, turned with it, drove a fist into the soft place below the man's ear.

Bone sang.

The knife flashed again; Julian trapped the wrist against the rock, elbow levered, body heavy. The blade clattered and went tidally into the dark.

Sofia scrabbled for her gun with her good hand. Each small movement hurt. The pistol lay two arm lengths away, just beyond dignity. She slid on knees and elbows, grabbed metal with wet fingers, turned, breath loud in her head.

The men became geometry—angles and

lines.

The assassin broke Julian's grip with an odd, beautiful twist, found the gun he'd dropped, brought it up. Julian shoved the inside of his forearm against the barrel and stapled it to the rock; the shot went into stone and screamed.

Smoke and rain made a bitter smell, electric and old.

Julian's face had become the one she only ever saw when it was him or death—absent of charm, absent of anything. He shifted weight, found the hinge of the other man's shoulder with his palm, and drove him backward.

The assassin's boot skidded on a skin of algae slicker than oil. For the first time, gravity remembered it owned him.

He went over the edge with the stupid grace of a falling thing, dropped, slammed, caught—a hand snaking around a root that had no business being there, fingers finding a purchase the width of a coin.

He hung.

The cliff wetly resented him. Waves tried to convince him he belonged to them now.

Julian rose, chest heaving, blood and rain sharing his face. He planted a boot at the edge, gun in his hand, triumph bright and raw.

"Where is she?" he shouted into the storm, voice skinned back to instinct. "Where is Mila?"

The assassin looked up. Water ran from his hood in rivers. The device in his left hand crackled with its too-calm voice, translation tinny under thunder. "Who?" it said, as if tasting the word.

Julian's mouth pulled into a savage grin. "Nowhere to go," he called down. "No gun. No hands. Talk or drown."

For a second, the world held. Sofia felt it—a coin spinning on edge between outcomes.

Then the man below moved. Not up. Not down. Sideways—hips twisting, core tightening, every inch of him learning leverage anew. His right leg scissored across the rock like a hook seeking meat.

Sofia saw it before Julian did and still too late.

"Jul—" she started.

The foot found Julian's ankle and wrenched. It wasn't a pull so much as a decision handed to bones. Julian's eyes went wide, a whole sentence in a single frame: *oh*.

Time elongated, elastic with horror. She watched the exact moment his balance left him. Watched the calculation in his face—

push back, fall forward, jump. Watched him choose grab and go.

He stumbled, fought, failed. The rock slicked under his boots as if it had been waiting all night for this joke.

Sofia lunged, fingers outstretched, the cut in her palm tearing open again. She caught his sleeve with the tips of two fingers; cloth slid; he reached up and there was a beat where they had each other by nothing but want.

And then they were gone—Julian and the man and gravity, all in one breath—tumbling off the cliff toward the black, boiling sea.

The storm roared like applause.

CHAPTER 20

Morning, but not the kind that forgives.

Wind still knifed along the cliff. Rain still came in ragged sheets that tasted of metal and salt. Sofia was so tired she felt hollowed out. Her right hand wouldn't stop bleeding; every pulse was a small hammer.

She stood on the rocks below the cliff—there, finally, after two hours of inching down goat paths that weren't paths at all. She had slipped, crawled, cut her palms, ripped her jeans, bled, and kept moving.

All night, she had searched.

Calling his name into a storm that ate sound. Waiting for a hand to break the surface. For a laugh. For a miracle.

Nothing.

The sea sprawled gray and endless, ribs of foam showing where the reef chewed it. The place where they'd gone over was a dirty bruise in the water, a churn of kelp and broken drift. If a body had surfaced in the night, the typhoon had taken it. If two bodies had not, the depths had.

The current here was a thief that didn't return what it stole.

She crouched on a wet slab and trembled from the inside out. The rock vibrated with the sea's breath; her bones vibrated to match it. She wrapped her good arm around her ribs, as if that could hold herself together.

Bezopasnost, she tried, but the word wouldn't take. The ritual that always calmed her felt like a joke with the punchline ripped out.

The storm had sagged a little. Not gone—never gone—but the wildest rage had burned through. Still dangerous. Still loud. Still a language of warning in the air, in the trees, in the hiss between wave and stone.

A horn cut through the wind—long, low, official. She lifted her head and saw lights out past the reef, stabbing white cones across the chop. White hulls. Rising and falling in violent rhythm. The Japanese Coast Guard.

More lights. More horns. Divers already zipped into black, their fins lined in reflective tape. A loudhailer crackled Japanese over the crash and suck of the sea; she caught pieces—*standing by, do not move, we are coming for you.*

She didn't move. Couldn't. The rock under

her was a tiny country and she its last citizen.

A figure stood braced at the bow of the nearest patrol boat, boots planted, coat snapping like a flag. NatashaKović. The set of her shoulders had always suggested a straightedge. Now it suggested a blade.

Even at this distance, Sofia felt the stare land: stern, assessing, angry. It made sense. They had never liked each other.

A smaller inflatable boat punched loose from the cutter and tore toward the rocks. Two officers in orange rain gear, helmets, visors. Rope lines at the ready. A diver crouched in the bow, gloved hand pointing, calibrating the tide's temper.

Sofia tried to stand and her legs argued. She compromised with a stagger, the world tilting, the cliff heaving up out of peripheral vision. The boat spun its stern to the rocks, timing the surge; two hands reached, found her under the arms, lifted her aboard in a single practiced motion. The impact of the deck jarred her spine like a punch.

"You are hurt," one of the cops said in careful English. "We take you to main ship. Please sit. Please hold."

She sat. She held.

The inflatable leapt and slammed, leapt

and slammed. They cut across the broken water toward the cutter where Natasha waited like a judge.

The moment her boots touched the big boat's nonskid deck, the crisp world of federal control closed around her—crew moving with purpose, a paramedic with a kit, a radio crackling concise commands. And Natasha, stepping forward, eyes blue and cold as glacier glass.

"We triangulated your satellite call," Natasha said over the wind without greeting. Her English, as always, was immaculate. "The safehouse. Then the car. Then nothing, until the Coast Guard pinged a distress beacon." She folded her arms. "Where is Julian?"

Sofia's mouth opened. A useless sound came out. She tried again. "Gone."

The word fell between them.

Natasha's eyes flashed, a bright hard thing. "Where is he?" Sharper, as if the answer might change if she cut it finer.

Sofia shook her head. She didn't trust her voice. The wind pressed at her back. Her hand throbbed.

"Gone," she said. "He went over the cliff. With the man who—" Her throat closed. She swallowed grit. "He went over."

Natasha stared at her as if Sofia had personally pitched him into the ocean. Fury moved under her face like weather over water. She stepped in so they were almost touching. "He is not a ball and this a fence, Costa. He does not go 'over.' Where is he?"

"Dead," Sofia said, because the other half of her mind needed the word said out loud to start believing it. "Dead."

Something flickered across Natasha's face then—an old pain she had buried under discipline and ambition and righteous superiority. Sofia watched her clamp it down and hate herself for watching. The moment passed; the blade returned.

"Divers in," Natasha barked without looking away, snapping orders in Japanese to the Coast Guard commander. Grid squares. Drift models. Rock shelves. Search windows. She wielded the storm map. A bosun repeated her calls; the deck came alive.

Sofia stood small and useless on her patch of deck, the world swinging under her, the wet sky trying to box her in. She felt raw and numb and so lonely she wanted to fold herself until she disappeared.

"You have a great many questions to answer," Natasha said finally, turning that straightedge face back on her. "Who killed those people at the station? Were you involved?"

Sofia stared at the water. It gave her nothing. "No," she said. It sounded like a translation from a language she no longer spoke.

"You have... let us call them unsavory connections," Natasha went on, the word deliberate. "Since you left Interpol. The Calderon twins. Velezzi's circles. You wade in dirty harbors and act surprised when you come up smelling of fuel."

Sofia's jaw worked. No sound. There were a thousand things to say, clever, cutting, true. She didn't have any of them. She had rain in her eyelashes and blood in her glove and a hole in her chest where a person belonged.

"After your parents' death," Natasha said more quietly, more cruel, "you broke. We both know it. You were emotionally unstable. You still are. This—" she flicked her fingers toward the cliff, toward the sea— "has your fingerprints on it whether or not you held a weapon."

Sofia looked down at her bandaged hand. The paramedic had stuck a dressing over the cut without asking; blood had seeped through anyway, making a darker starburst that spread with each heartbeat. It throbbed in time with the engines.

She did not answer. She had no spare energy for defense. She could not make her throat shape the words she would have liked to say: that Julian made his own choices; that he could not be contained by anyone's caution; that he would have laughed at her for trying to stop him. That he would have gone after her the same way and expected her to forgive him for it after.

The searchlights swung. Divers vanished into gray. The sea flexed and settled and flexed again. Ropes creaked. Radios snapped in and out of clarity. The rain thinned to needles and then thickened again as another band of weather shouldered through.

She watched Natasha point, command, carve the chaos into tasks. She watched the boats reposition on the swell. She watched hope perform its ritual so that the body could continue to stand up.

The water did not give Julian back.

She prayed without words, the way you do when the person you're talking to is either everywhere or nowhere. She stood with her head bent against the wind and asked for something small: a sign. A sleeve. A scrap. A reason not to believe the last thirty minutes of her life were the last thirty minutes of his. The gray sea shrugged.

Minutes lost their edges. The world narrowed to a circle of metal deck, a circle of cold light, her breath fogging and vanishing, her hand pulsing pain. People moved around her and not through her. She existed like a buoy exists—anchored by something she couldn't see, rocked by forces she couldn't fight.

"I will be asking you again," Natasha said, voice closer, voice softer now in a way that wasn't mercy. "Again and again, if necessary. If this touches Interpol's work, if this touches my work, I will take you apart until I know what you know."

Sofia nodded once. She was too tired to disagree. Too sad to do anything but accept every punishment she could not stop anyway.

The waves eased a fraction. The white water curled a little less savagely around the rocks. The wind lost a note and gained another. The divers surfaced in pairs, shook their heads, went down again, dwindled to ghosts under the surface.

Sofia's head dipped. Came up. Dipped. Her body did not belong to her anymore; it belonged to the storm and the work it had done on her.

She tried the ritual one last time,

a whisper she barely heard. "Bezopasnost. Seguridad. Ān quán." Safety, safety, safety. The words were stones she placed in a line. They didn't make a path. They just fell where they fell.

She felt the world tilt, then soften. Her hand was a drum. Her knees forgot to lock. The deck came up, slow and then very fast.

The last thing she saw was the gray water, flat as a closed eye. The last thing she heard was the engine's steady heart and Natasha's voice.

She let her head fall. The darkness opened its mouth and she went into it.

CHAPTER 21

The world came back in squares—ceiling tiles, pale and exact; a fluorescent hum steady as a metronome; the thin antiseptic bite of hospital air. Pain announced itself from her right hand first, a hot, pulsing star under clean gauze. Everything else felt floaty and bruised.

Someone sat in the visitor's chair, hat brim low. A white fisherman's cap. A white mustache that looked like something a theater would keep in a box.

He was reading a newspaper upside down.

Sofia blinked. The mustache twitched. The paper righted itself.

"You look like a woman who could use a less fluorescent light," the man said, carefully, in a Portuguese that had been ironed flat for export. The voice was familiar.

She closed her eyes, opened them again. The disguise didn't improve.

He leaned forward; the cap shadow slipped higher. Gray eyes, tired but sharp. A long face mapped in sun-lines. The faint, comforting scent of ink and lemon balm tea, like afternoons in a cramped shop where the dust motes knew her name.

"Nuno?" she whispered.

The white mustache loosened at one corner, then surrendered its will to gravity. He caught it with a fingertip, sighed, and pressed it back on at a jaunty angle that fooled no one.

"In the flesh," he said, softer now, his real cadence returning—Lisbon vowels warmed by old habit. A tweed coat sat on his shoulders even here; inside pockets bulged with folded papers. His salt-and-pepper hair was tied back in a low knot beneath the cap. He looked very much like a man who had been tidy his whole life and had decided to rebel by gluing a pipe cleaner to his face.

She felt the panic flare up her throat. "You can't be here," she said, hoarse. "Natasha—"

"Does not like me," he finished, with the faintest smile that never reached his eyes. "I had noticed. She has chased me out of better rooms."

"She's gone after you before to get to me." Sofia's breath quickened. The monitors tattled. "If she sees you—"

He lifted a hand, palm out, peace. "I came the long way. The chatter on Interpol channels was… loud." His mouth worked. "I am sorry, menina." He said it very simply, and the room tilted.

Julian. The fact of it was a black weight on her ribs. For one breath, it slid and crushed and she couldn't pull air around it. She turned her face away; the ceiling blurred. The small, stupid Seiko on her wrist ticked as if all this were normal.

Nuno reached for the call button, then didn't. He was good at not pushing the thing he wanted to push. "I brought nothing helpful," he said softly, as if confessing. "Only my bad company and a mustache I am beginning to suspect was made for a child's school play."

Her voice came out as a rasp. "Did Isabella Calderon help you with that?"

A reluctant nod. "She gave me pointers," he admitted, as if this were the most shameful thing he'd ever done. "But I think the glue is from a time when glue still believed in duty."

Sofia tried to smile. It hurt. Her hand throbbed in time with the incremental climb of grief.

He watched her, then looked past her to whatever was coming down the hall and decided to be normal. He was very good at normal. "Lisbon is quieter without you," he said. "The tram still grinds like a bored dragon. The tourists drink my kombucha and pretend to like it. I think they are lying, but lying politely." He scratched at the crooked mustache. "A German professor tried to sell me my own first edition of Saramago last week. I bought it back because I admired his confidence."

"Nuno."

"I retired," he said, as if she had asked. "Officially. Paperwork and everything. They gave me a pen too heavy to use and a speech too long to hear. The shop has mice with opinions." He tilted his head at her bandaged hand. "How are you?"

She stared at him. The honest answer sat in her chest like a stone she couldn't lift. "Empty," she said, because anything else would be a lie she'd have to remember.

He nodded once, something in his face tightening the way sailcloth does when wind finds it. "Have you made progress on Valezzi?" he asked, so gently the question almost sounded like weather.

Sofia looked at him and didn't. *Valezzi sends her regards,* the assassin's device had whispered. Nuno's careful, stupid mustache hovered in her peripheral vision like a white moth. If she said it, she would put him in the crosshairs of that voice. If she said it, he would stay.

"No," she said, and watched the lie fall down between them and shatter. She could not make herself pick up the pieces.

His eyes softened in a way she had seen twice in ten years. He reached into his coat and produced—God help him—a small amber bottle. "Kombucha," he said, a ghost of pride crossing his face. "Ginger. Terrible. But it is alive. That seems like the bar today."

She laughed once, a dry, broken bark that surprised both of them.

Silence after. The hospital spoke in beeps and rubber soles and murmur. Outside, wind scraped its knuckles along the windows. He told her a little nothing—a woman in Alfama who fed the pigeons too much bread, a bookseller's argument over whether Pessoa was one ghost or seven—and she understood him perfectly. He was offering her time where time did not hurt.

The thought landed mid-sentence: *He is here. With me.* And the panic that had been flickering steady suddenly found oxygen.

"Go," she said, the word harsher than she intended. "You have to leave."

He blinked. "Sofia—"

"Now." She tried to sit up; her hand screamed. "You can't be here. Natasha will — And the man—" Her throat closed on it. "Please. Please go. I don't want you here."

He absorbed the blow like a man who had sailed in bad weather. It still struck. His mouth compressed; the lines at his eyes deepened. "I have liked many people in the abstract," he said quietly. "I like you in the practical." He stood anyway, because she'd asked.

She hated herself for what she said next and said it anyway, because love that stays alive learns to be cruel. "Go, Nuno. Hide. Don't come back."

He stepped close despite her words and gave her a stiff, awkward hug—his version of an embrace, all elbows and resolve. He patted her head like she was six and had skinned a knee. "I will be back soon," he murmured into her hair.

"Don't," she said into his coat. "Please don't."

He held a breath, let it go, nodded. The white mustache slid again. He caught it and almost smiled. "Eat something," he said, an old reflex, then turned, straightened the cap, and left by the same improbable path he'd used to come in.

The door clicked. The room remembered

it was a room.

Sofia pressed the heels of her hands to her eyes until sparks lived there. She let two sobs out because they were bigger than her and then caught the rest because there was no point in spilling when nothing would be mopped. Her mother's voice came—soft Portuguese in a kitchen that always smelled faintly of oranges, hands guiding smaller hands. *When the feeling is too big, filha, put it somewhere that can hold it. A tune. A word. A task. Then come back to it when your feet are on the ground.*

A tune. A word. A task.

Bezopasnost. The syllables found edges again. *Seguridad.* A little steadier. *Ān quán.* She breathed them like steps on a stair.

A task: **Mila**.

She looked at her bandaged palm. The stitches bit when she flexed—sharp, clean pain. Good. It told her she was still in here.

If she stayed, Natasha would peel her like a label. There were likely police at the end of the hall already, a bored officer with a clipboard and a list of questions printed too small. Interpol would circle. They would point her at their definition of useful and call it mercy.

She couldn't stay.

She rolled carefully to one side. The IV line had a clever little latch; hospitals trusted patients less than locks did. She pressed and slid and freed herself with a small, guilty pop. The monitor complained in a steady tone until she found the button that asked it to consider silence. Her clothes—dried by someone else, folded into a neat rectangle—sat on a chair under a disposable blanket. She dressed slowly, biting the inside of her cheek when the sleeve snagged her stitches.

Shoes. She found a pair of hospital slippers and hated them on sight. The coast outside the window wore tatters of cloud and storm, but the rage had passed to another island. She could hear emergency helicopters someplace far off, looking for what the sea didn't intend to give.

She eased the door open, listened. Footsteps going away. A nurse's laugh that meant *tired but coping*. The murmur of a TV at the nurses' station turned low to make people behave. She slipped into the corridor with the same casual posture with which she had walked out of a dozen countries that had decided to keep her.

At the station, a young nurse in pink scrubs was filling out a form with a pen that clicked too loudly; Sofia could hear her counting patients under her breath in Japanese, a cadence she knew meant *overloaded*. A uniformed cop sat three chairs down, legs splayed, tapping at his phone with the concentration of a man trying to beat a level before someone asked him to stand up. His rain poncho hung to drip on the floor, forming a small, irregular lake that reflected the ceiling light.

Sofia smiled with her eyes and kept moving. If challenged, she had a sentence ready in polite, precise Japanese about needing fresh air for nausea, about the bathroom, about a call she had to make to her embassy. People believed what fit the shape of their day.

They didn't look up.

The elevator chimed. She took the stairs instead, one flight, then another, hand sliding the railing only because her knees thought about betraying her. On the ground floor, the automatic doors sighed open to a world washed clean and left raw. The parking lot glimmered with puddles that still remembered the typhoon's feet. Palms leaned at new angles. The sky was the color of a bruise that had begun to fade.

A taxi idled at the curb, driver smoking out the window, radio murmuring the morning's damage reports. She walked straight to it because hesitation reads as guilt in any language.

"Minami Ridge," she said through the window in Japanese, voice steady enough to pass. "Building Three."

The driver glanced at her bandaged hand, then at the hospital behind her, then back to the road. He reached to snap his meter without commentary. "Hai."

She slid into the back seat and let the plastic seat cover squeak under her. As they pulled away, the hospital fell behind with the soft indifference of institutions. She did not look back.

The taxi nosed into a town that had been simplified by wind—fewer signs, fewer branches. Blue tarps bloomed on roofs. People stood in doorways and took inventory of what the night had left behind. The road climbed in a gentle spiral toward the ridge. Far below, the sea was a rough sheet, ironed in places by sunlight.

She pressed her bandaged palm against her thigh to quiet the throb and made herself rehearse the task like lines in a play. **Daichi Nakamura. Minami Ridge. Building 3. Unit 402.** The admin account pinging the call server at hours when storms strangle bandwidth. *You were off the island,* she would say, casually. *And yet your workstation was busy.* She would ask it the way Nuno had taught her: as if the answer were already graciously given.

Julian would have gone. He would have burned himself down to ash to get to a door Mia might be behind. He had, in fact. It was her turn to be fire without smoke.

She watched the ridge rise ahead, the building blocks of Minami's concrete teeth showing between bowed trees. Her breath shortened, not with fear; with a thing that had purpose in it.

If love had a shape she could wear without collapsing under it, it looked like this: a woman in a taxi with a bandaged hand, going to keep a promise the sea had tried to drown.

"Almost," the driver said, glancing in the mirror.

"Thank you," Sofia answered, and meant it.

CHAPTER 22

The intercom crackled like a seashell. Sofia pressed the button and kept her voice small, contrite Japanese, the kind tenants recognize as "delivery that forgot to call ahead."

"Sumimasen… ame de…," she said, rain excuse at the ready.

A buzz. The lobby door hiccuped open on its magnet. She slipped through.

Minami Ridge smelled of wet concrete and boiled rice. Fluorescent tubes buzzed over a vestibule of mailboxes and a laminated evacuation map the typhoon had peeled at the corners. A security camera blinked a red dot above the elevator, staring past her shoulder with machine indifference. She lifted her chin, made herself a forgettable shape.

Fourth floor. Unit 402.

She took the stairs, counting landings. Her right palm throbbed beneath its neat gauze.

At 402 she knocked three times, then

once, knuckles a metronome. She held still, listening—the building's breath, the petulant drip of a downspout, someone's TV murmuring a game show laugh track two doors over.

Silence at the door, except... not. The latch was lazy; the jamb not quite married to the frame. The handle gave under her fingers.

A sliver of the hallway across the building showed in the sheen of the peephole. Two floors below, a door banged. A voice carried up the stairwell in quick, official Japanese, edges clipped: "Call came from this floor —commotion—unit four-oh-two." Another voice answered, lower, calmer: "Keisatsu desu. Check procedure. No hero." Police. Coming up, deliberate feet.

Her skin prickled cold. She slid inside 402 and brought the door quietly to, turned the lock with a prayer she did not know how to say.

Empty air. A room paused mid-breath.

"Daichi Nakamura?" she called softly into the entryway, the sound swallowed by thin walls and thicker carpet. No answer.

Move.

It was a small, clean space, the kind of rental that pretended at personality with cheap art. Shoebox entry lined with placid slippers. A galley kitchen to the right—bright, steel, polite. The living area had a low couch and a glass-topped table and a balcony drowned in beaded rain. The glass top glittered wrong: fracture.

Shards lay on the floor like a constellation, spread in an arc that pointed—not random scatter, but a trajectory—toward the bedroom hall. The largest pieces had crawled farther, riding water that had found them when the typhoon shouldered its way inside. The carpet there was darker, a rain map.

She passed the kitchen. The knife block had a gap, third slot from the left. Santoku missing. Her stomach went cold.

At the end of the hall a door was cracked. Air moved in it, the whisper of a room that had an open window. The hairs on her arms rose.

She pressed the door with two fingers.

A man lay on the bed, on top of the duvet. Mid-thirties, hair cut practical, a neat accountant's watch on his left wrist, a tan line where a ring had been often enough to matter.

A kitchen knife stood in his chest like a blunt, ugly flag.

Sofia's brain did that old, clean thing where it put a grid over the world. Each square a note. Each note a fact.

Window open—curtain lifting and laying, lifting and laying. The sill was wet. Rain had tracked from the window to the bed. The carpet at the threshold had soaked and then dried in a tide line. Long time open. Through the storm.

Smell: iron, rain, damp plaster. Under it, a ghost of citrus cleaner. Someone had wiped at something and then quit.

Blood. A lot. Not the ballistic splatter of a professional's certainty, not the tidy oval of a single precise thrust and surgical silence. This was mess: slung arcs on the bedframe where arms thrashed, a dark smear along the wall at shoulder height, a drip-line across the floor that said someone dragged a blade or a hand, then stumbled.

The wound itself was deep but off-center, slightly upward angle—shorter assailant, or one who lunged from below in panic.

His hands told the rest. Palms scored with crescent cuts. Back of the left hand raked by four parallel scratches, defensive, a scrabble against steel. A nick along the ring finger— a ring ripped off then or earlier? The nails ragged with carpet fibers. He had fought.

The knife. From the kitchen. Brought nothing. Took whatever was at hand. Amateur.

Her mouth said it before her brain did. "This was personal," she murmured. The storm pushed the curtain inward as if to nod.

A hush fell in the hall outside the apartment, then a polite, practiced knock. "Keisatsu desu! Akenasai!" Police. Open the door. A second knock: louder. "We received a report—"

Sofia glanced back toward the entry. Saw the lens of the door camera like a small black pupil looking in. Her stomach sank. They had a picture of her already.

She made herself breathe. The grid stayed on the room. Details filed themselves: a scuff on the headboard at shoulder height where someone's heel had slammed, a lamp on the floor, shade crushed as if a hand had used it to rise. The closet door stood ajar. Inside: a man's shirts organized by color, edges aligned. A small toolkit on the floor with a screwdriver missing. Not useful now. A laundry basket of clean clothes, uncreased.

She scanned the nightstand. A cracked phone face-down, a cheap charging cable pulled from the wall by force. No wallet. No keys. Either the killer took them or he—or *she* —left with the ordinary calm of someone who belonged. Calm enough to lock the door? It had been loose, not latched. They fled fast. Or had entered hastily.

Sofia leaned in for what her old training called the *gift*—the single oddity that did not fit the script.

There: a smudge on the open window's handle. Not blood. Rust? No. Reddish-brown, thin. Clay. The sort you get under nails from a plant pot. The balcony bore climbing greenery; a trellis on one side linked 402's railing to 302's tiny herb jungle, stems torn, string snapped. Someone had come or gone that way, during a typhoon.

Not the assassin with the robotic voice. He'd been with them on the cliff. Not Yakuza— they brought knives from home and friends to carry you to the car. Not Interpol. Not Valezzi's people. The violence was frantic, not cold; the blade choice was opportunistic; the aftermath sloppy. This was an amateur. Which meant motive was not money or orders.

"Something personal," she said under her breath. "Not whales. Not currents."

A fist boomed against the front door, then another. "Akenasai!" A key scraped uselessly at her lock. The tone of the voices sharpened from procedure to urgency. They were getting angry. Or afraid.

Her mind flipped through faces—Hiro's flush when he spoke of Mila; Emi's quick, defensive eyes; the old fisherman's reluctance. The grid held up a mirror and showed her own. What if—her breath hitched—what if they had it wrong from the beginning?

What if Mila's disappearance did not belong to the ocean at all?

Personal.

What if it belonged to a kitchen and a fight and a person?

The thought slid into place with a click that felt like a lock accepting the right key. Horror chased it—fast—like wind after a door slams.

No time to finish it. No time to be right.

She crossed to the balcony. Outside, the trellis swayed, a drunk metronome. The rain had thinned to an obstinate spit, wind still combing the building from right to left. Four floors up. A string of plant pots clung to their brackets. Below, a narrow strip of communal garden, then a tarmac lane slick as glass.

Behind her, the police pounded again. A radio crackled. "Breaker bar," someone said in Japanese. "Get the manager."

She shouldered the balcony door open and leaned into gray. The trellis held, creaking. Her bandaged hand made a small, furious noise. She wrapped her left hand around the wood and tested her weight, then her right, carefully, the stitches complaining like old men.

"On three," she told herself, and didn't wait for three.

She swung a leg over the railing, found a crossbar with her foot, and let her body drop into the logic of climbing. The wood was wet and slippery; her shoes had to find conviction where there was none. She pushed away from the building to avoid the drainpipe, to keep her weight on the verticals. The bandage took weight and screamed, white pain flaring; she made her muscles into one long apology and went down anyway.

The door behind her shuddered. A lock surrendered its one job. A shout: "Police!"

Sofia kept moving, eyes on the next rung, the next, the next. The curtain in the bedroom snapped once like a hand saying goodbye.

She climbed.

CHAPTER 23

Night had stitched the island back together with tarps and rope and willpower. Streets still wore the storm—branches slick with salt, tatami mats airing over railings, a crescent of somebody's zinc roof folded like a toy on the curb. The air smelled like wet copper and diesel and bruised hibiscus.

Sofia waited in the lee of a vending machine that still blinked cheerful beverages nobody wanted. Her bandaged hand throbbed in time with the faint buzz of the neon *OPEN* sign two doors down. Across the narrow street stood the building she'd already been inside once this afternoon while the landlord argued with the police on the fourth floor. She had seen enough then to know what she needed to see now.

He had loved her. Not a crush you could carry around in a work lanyard, not the professional admiration that makes late nights easier. Love with rituals. Love with taxonomy. The extra mug on the dish rack that matched Mila's at the station. A whale's fluke watercolored on cheap paper and tacked over his desk. No crime in any of it. But a line crossed so often it had become a groove.

A taxi eased by, tires whispering through wet. Sofia pulled her hood forward and breathed.

She had burned her last favor to get here. Called in through a relay that should've been retired, said the old words to the right bored operator who still owed Nuno. A handset clicked, an old modem hissed. Then: a ping. The phone she wanted drew a neat blue dot on a map.

Nuno couldn't help. He'd stepped off the chessboard and into a bookshop. Julian—her throat closed even in thought. Interpol would not help her again after tonight. She was stealing the last sugar from that cupboard.

She watched the doorway. She knew who had taken Mila. Knew who had made the call to Barcelona and turned a brother into a weapon. Knew who had stabbed a man in a bed with a kitchen knife when a winter sea shook the windows.

A jealous lover made more sense than a syndicate. A stalker read more truthfully than a cartel. They had looked for a dragon and found a dog with a taste for blood.

Footsteps came from around the corner,

tapping at a careful pace—avoid the deep puddle, step over the bent sign, watch the loose tile. He turned into the spill of neon: rectangular glasses fogged at the edges, slight shoulders under a rain jacket, hair pulled back in a short ponytail that had seen more ocean wind than salon. Hiro.

Shorter than the men who had tried to scare them in the garden. The angle of a knife from below made fresh sense.

He saw her at the same instant she stepped out. Stopped dead in the middle of the sidewalk. Mouth opened. Stared.

"Costa-san?" he said, voice gone thin. "You —are you—?" His gaze dropped to the bandage, the rain-flattened hair, the salt-stiff jacket. "I heard what happened to your friend. It's on the news. I am… I'm so sorry."

She said nothing. Watched him.

His pupils were wide—not only from the dark. His pulse ticked in his throat, rabbit-fast. Shoulders slightly raised—fear and a little guilt, but that was a region, not a street. His voice sat too high, a half step sharp. He kept his hands visible, palms out from his sides as if approaching a spooked horse.

She moved a step closer until the neon painted both of them a soft and stupid blue. "I know what you did," she said, even and flat.

He blinked. "What... I don't—"

"I know it was you," she continued, before his protest could find a shape. "The calls to her. The calls to *him*. The backdoor into the station logs. Using your colleague's credentials. Your phone called Barcelona. *We're going to take her*, you said. You wanted to scare a brother the way you were scaring her."

Hiro shook his head at each clause as if he could erase consonants by motion alone. He took a step back like the wall behind him had a promise in it, then found it with his shoulder and leaned, as if bracing could keep truth from happening.

"I..." He swallowed, and the tendon in his neck jumped. "I loved her," he said, the word landing wrong in the air and true in his mouth. "I really loved her. I have never—there is no one like her." He looked at the street, the bent sign, anywhere but her. "The way she looked at the water and saw sentences. The way the children—" His voice broke. "I know this is nothing you want to hear."

Sofia's face did not move. Her hand throbbed. She could still feel, in the bones that mattered, the moment Julian's weight left this world.

"Is Mila dead?" she asked.

He stared at her, wet and wrecked. "No,"

he said, and for the first time his eyes met hers. "I didn't hurt her. I did love her—yes. Too much. Maybe. I wanted her found because I wanted her safe. I checked call logs. I did that. I was worried she was—" He flushed, shame a heat you could see. "I was worried she was dating someone. That is stupid. I know. I should not have done it. But I didn't call your friend in Barcelona. I didn't threaten him. I didn't lure her away. I would never." His hands came up higher as if to show he wasn't hiding blood. "You have to believe me."

She wanted not to. She counted his tells like rosary beads: pupils, pulse, pitch, posture. The old machine in her brain spun and clicked and threw up an answer she didn't like.

He was telling the truth.

A cold ribbon laid itself along her spine. If not Hiro, then—

"You said you thought she was dating someone," Sofia said, keeping her voice level. "Why?"

His shoulders hunched. "Flowers," he said. "Left on her desk. Twice. Maybe three times. I saw a note once. I didn't read it," he added quickly, shame making the words hurry. "It had a heart. Like a... like a teenager would do." He looked smaller saying it.

Sofia held him in silence a heartbeat

longer than was polite and a heartbeat less than was cruel. He filled the gap with worry.

"She's not dead, is she?" he asked, voice small. "Please. Costa-san. I—if she is—"

Sofia's mind ran tight circles, then spooled out like a cast net and came back with something wriggling. *Did you show anyone how to access those logs? Would anyone else have had your phone?*

"Did you ever share access?" she asked. "The call server. Your phone. Your colleague's credentials."

He hesitated. Not long. Long enough. "Only the students who help me," he said. "Sometimes I let them use my machine for simulations when the lab is full. Once or twice I wrote the login on a card." He flinched at the admission. "It was with other cards. Project passwords. Someone could have seen. But I don't think—"

She didn't hear the end. The click in her head was so loud it turned the street down. A heart drawn in marker on a hand. The screen saver of Mila on her phone. A student who moved like a fuse.

Sofia's body went very still. Cold filled the spaces grief had hollowed out.

"I'm sorry," she said, almost

automatically. "For accusing you. I need your help. Where is she?"

"Mila?" he asked, confused.

"Not Mila." She took a step closer; he flinched, then held his ground. "Emi."

It made sense now. The small heart on Emi's wrist. The lockscreen of her phone, a smiling picture of Mila laughing over a tide pool with children

His face did a series of small things that ended in stunned. "I... I don't know," he said. "She left the night you and Julian did. In the storm. She texted me that she was going to check roof damage at her apartment. That was... that was a lie?" He shook his head, trying to reorder a story he had only been given the wrong pages of. "She did not come back."

Sofia saw it as if she'd been there: the kitchen knife missing from its block, the rain driving sideways through a window. A short, desperate fight in a stranger's rented bedroom. A trellis shaking like a ladder. An amateur. A heart on a note.

"She was gone to kill your colleague," Sofia said, the words grim and quiet. "The one whose login she saw in your stack. She thought he would point to her or to Mila or to... something. Or she thought he knew. She tried to tie it off and made a mess. We need to find her."

Hiro's mouth opened and shut. "If she hurt Mila—" He stopped, swallowed, steadied. "If she hurt anyone—I'll do what I can."

"Call her," Sofia said. "Now. Ask her where she is. Tell her you need help at the lab. Tell her the servers are down. Something she can't resist fixing. Can you do that?"

He looked at her like a man stepping into a deep pool, not knowing if it was water or glass. Then he nodded.

He reached into his jacket for his phone. It buzzed in his hand before he had it all the way out, screen lighting his wet glasses, lighting the worry carved into his face.

The name on the display bloomed bright as a wound.

CHAPTER 24

Emi's spiky blue hair lay plastered to her skull, darkened to ink by salt and rain. Mascara had run in two crooked ladders down her cheeks and dried there, a child's watercolor left out in a squall. The dinghy lifted and dropped, lifted and dropped, the sea shouldering it like an impatient ox. She gripped the oars and pulled until her shoulders burned.

Don't look back. She looked back.

Mila lay in the stern, wrists bound behind her with orange line from the lab, knees drawn up, a blanket thrown over her legs that did nothing against the cold. Her hair was wet rope against her neck. She shivered in small, stubborn tremors, the kind you get when you decide not to give anyone the satisfaction of seeing you shake.

"Why won't you just love me," Emi hissed, the words starting small and swelling, "the way I love you?"

The ocean took her question and did not return it.

It had been three days of trying to show Mila how perfect this could be. Three days of tea and gentle hands and forced smiles and explanations and the careful retelling of moments as if a better version existed if you said it right. Three days of brushing damp hair back, of arranging shells on the windowsill of the hut, of saying *see? see?* as if proof were a necklace you could clasp for someone. Three days of *I'm helping you* and *they don't understand you* and *we don't need them*. Three days of Mila looking at her with that steady, sad gaze that felt like a door closing without sound.

Emi's breath hitched. "I have done everything," she said to the waves, then to Mila. "I know you. I know how the water looks in your eyes when the humpbacks breach. I know the way you hum when you think no one is listening. I know what you keep in your left desk drawer. I know how you take the tea the old man gives you at the dock. So why—why—"

She slammed the oar into its cradle and twisted for the stern in a sudden, furious lunge. Her hand—split knuckles, a bright crescent of raw skin across the palm—came down in a slap that cracked the night. Mila's head swung to the side and back. She did not make a sound.

Emi's breath tore out of her, and she

clutched the injured hand to her chest. The skin there still remembered a different night—rain gone sideways, glass everywhere like teeth, a kitchen that smelled of steel and fear, her own breath a saw in her throat. She had slipped across the trellis and into the open window with her heart in her mouth and the storm shoving at her back. She had told herself there was no choice. He would ruin it. He would tell. He would break the fragile bridge she was building. She had been so sure until the moment the knife was in her hand and the world narrowed to a point and afterwards everything was red and too loud and she could not hear her name in her own head.

"It was the only way," she said out loud, voice bright and brittle. "It was. You know that. He—he would have—" She couldn't find the right ending. She hadn't found one in that room, either. The memory made a small sound inside her and kept making it.

Mila twisted her shoulders a little, the line scraping against itself. Her voice, when it came, was hoarse. "Emi," she said, gentle like you talk to a skittish dog, "please."

"I'm the only one who—" Emi swallowed, hard, and shoved the oars back into the water. The next pull was wild, then steadied. The wind had slacked since afternoon, but the swell still carried the memory of typhoon hands. Far out, beyond the reefs, low clouds bruised purple—another storm building its spine. Not as bad as the last two. Bad enough for a boat that was mostly wood and wish.

"We were meant," Emi said, almost conversational, breath coming in sawed pieces. "You know that. I know you know that. You just—" She flung another look over her shoulder. "Why won't you say it? Why won't you just say it and make it stop?"

Mila held her gaze. There was pity there and a thousand things that were not the thing Emi wanted, and that made everything inside Emi jitter and slide. Mila's mouth opened and closed. She shook her head, tiny, not defiance —grief.

"You would never hurt me," Emi said quickly, as if reciting something that had been true all along. "Even if you could get out of that—" she flicked her chin at the line—"you wouldn't. You wouldn't run." Her throat worked. "You're good. That's why I—" She cut the sentence off because the rest would scorch.

The phone in her jacket trilled, a thin insect buzz against her ribs. Emi flinched like she'd been touched by a live wire. She dug it out with clumsy fingers. The screen washed her face blue. HIRO, all caps, neat, familiar.

Her thumb hovered.

The dinghy rocked. The sea made small, insistent bird sounds against the hull. Mila watched her with a kind of stillness that made Emi's bones ache.

The phone trilled again. HIRO. She could see him in her mind: glasses fogged, careful hands, that way he said Mila's name like it was a coordinate. He would ask questions with that soft voice and then he would call someone else and then they would come and they would take and they would break and this small, pure thing would be spoiled like everything else people touched.

She swiped the call away and it returned as if hope itself were on the line. Her thumb trembled. Her breathing went ragged.

"Maybe," she whispered, almost to herself, almost to the sea. "Maybe he could… maybe—" She imagined telling him.

The phone hummed a third time. The screen lit her pupils wide. In the stern, Mila closed her eyes, like a prayer.

"No," Emi said, and the word was a door slamming from the inside.

She wound her arm back and threw. The phone made a clean, bright sound as it hit the water, a discrete *plip* swallowed immediately by the swell. She watched the circle of light sink until it was nothing, and then she could not see even where it had been.

"There's no point," she said, to silence, or to herself. "Not where we're going."

She set the oars again and pulled. The rhythm steadied. The island softened behind them into a low, dark shape, then a suggestion, then an absence. Wind stroked the little hairs at the back of her neck. In the far distance thunder rolled.

"We'll go far," Emi said quietly. The words sounded like a story a child would tell in a flashlight circle. "Until there's nothing human left. And then we won't have to choose. We'll go together. Like we were supposed to." She smiled, and it was a torn thing. "It's romantic. Don't you think?"

Mila shivered. "Emi," she said again, so soft it barely made it past her lips. Not pleading. Not bargaining. Just a name carried on a breath.

Emi looked back, and for a heartbeat she saw it the way someone kind would: two people in a terrible little boat under a huge sky, one girl with blue hair and sore hands, another woman tied and shivering and still somehow making space in her mouth for the name of the person who might kill her.

"It has to be this," Emi said, and put her back into the next pull, and the next.

They slid toward the storm on the horizon that would peel itself open into rain by midnight. The dinghy made the small, stubborn sounds of something that did not know it was fragile. Emi counted strokes to keep from counting other things. Twelve. Thirteen. Fourteen. She did not look back again. She did not need to. She could feel Mila there the way you feel a star you can't see—a true thing, bright behind a cloud.

The island sank behind them and became an idea. The dark ahead became plan. Emi paddled, jaw set, eyes burning, and told the water the ending she had chosen.

They would go out until there was no more out to go. And then, like the lovers they were meant to be, they would slip below the world and let it keep spinning without them.

CHAPTER 25

Hiro's thumbs flew and failed, flew and failed. The little green call bar vanished, came back, vanished again. Rain freckled the windshield in a mean, intermittent spit, leftover spray from gutters that hadn't relearned where water should go. The wipers squeaked like mice.

"Does she usually ignore your calls?" Sofia asked, watching the intersection, then the rearview.

"No." Hiro didn't look up. "Never."

Something slid into place in Sofia's chest. She eased the borrowed kei car off the main road, let a police cruiser drift past in her rearview in a slow, suspicious glide, then turned again and kept turning until the siren's hum was swallowed by wind.

"She's on the water," Sofia said, not as a guess but as a taste in her mouth. "We need a trace."

"I don't have that kind of access," Hiro said, soft. "Not… legally."

Neither did she. Not anymore. The last favor was gone with the last blue dot on a map. She looked down at her bandaged hand, flexed until the stitches bit. A tune, a word, a task.

She scrolled to a number she had sworn she would not use again.

Nuno answered on the first ring, which meant he'd been holding the phone. "Menina," he said, and made it sound like a prayer he hadn't planned to say. His voice wore a softness first, then something like hurt.

"I'm sorry," she said, first thing. "I was —" She couldn't find the right noun for the hospital, for the cliff, for any of it. "I need you," she said instead. "I need a trace."

"Of course," he said, and if hurt lived anywhere in him it went to the back room and closed the door. Only then did she hear the Kombucha. His words came half a second late, stitched together with a lazy seam. "Give me the number. And a tower. And a prayer to Saint Antenna. I have… some ideas."

Sofia rattled off Emi's details, the model, carrier, habits—everything she remembered from confiscating the phones in the safe house. "It'll take a few minutes," he said. "Talk to me while I sin."

She drove aimlessly through streets still tattooed by the storm—downed lines like sleeping snakes, palm fronds heaped in neat pyramids by hands that needed something to do. A rooster strutted through a puddle as if it had always been a mirror.

"Do you have equipment?"

"Give me—ah. Give me... two minutes."

She hung a left into a lane that dead-ended at a shrine gate half toppled by wind, reversed, nosed out again. A patrol car reappeared behind them—different unit, same watchfulness. She let it go by, breathing through her teeth, and counted to twenty in Portuguese.

Her phone hummed. "The signal went walking," Nuno said without greeting. "Then it learned to swim." The Kombucha rounded the words; the mind behind them was a scalpel. "Out to sea. Last handshake puts her—one-point-eight nautical miles east-southeast of Kagami-shima. Bearing one-two-seven from the south pier. Moving slow. Then... nothing. Dead phone."

"Shut off?"

"Or baptized." He exhaled in her ear. "The weather, minha filha—"

"I see it," she said, and she did. The horizon had put on a darker coat. The new storm had shoulders.

"Nuno," she said, softer. "Thank you."

He made a noise that might once have been a laugh. "Bring her back," he said. "Bring you back." Then, quieter, the hurt peeking through the door and closing it again, "And try not to shout at old men in disguises."

The line went dead.

Sofia threw the kei car toward the harbor; Hiro braced both hands on the dash without complaint. They skid to a stop beneath battered floodlights. The south wharf looked like a jaw with teeth knocked out—two boats snapped like breadsticks against the concrete, one capsized and still crying bubbles, one riding low and stubborn behind a jungle of extra lines.

The fishermen were gone or counting damage elsewhere. Keys dangled from an ignition.

Sofia took the invitation.

The borrowed boat coughed awake, then caught, diesel. The wheel felt too light in her hands, but it listened. Hiro stood beside her with his feet wide and his throat working, the color gone thin along his cheekbones.

"Have you done this before?" he asked.

"Once," Sofia said. "On the Bosphorus at midnight. The current was worse and the tea was better."

He blinked. Then nodded because what else could you do.

The pier fell away. The town flattened itself against the hill like a cat in a narrow doorway. Out past the breakwater, the sea found its old self. Swells moved under them. Far off, a line of cloud rolled its shoulders and began to walk toward them.

Sofia pushed the throttle; the bow lifted and slapped down, lifted and slapped. Spray hit her face like needles; she tasted salt and old metal. Hiro's phone light flickered across a paper chart as he traced Nuno's bearing, hands shaking but accurate. "One-two-seven from here," he said. "Then we adjust for drift."

"Then we improvise," Sofia said.

The last of the day had drained out of the sky. The sea took what color it wanted and kept it. They ran in a gray that was almost black, horizon a black scar.

"Emi," Hiro said, half to himself, half to the motor. "Please."

Then, off their starboard, a shape. Small. Wrong for the water. A smudge that rose and fell and rose again.

"There," Sofia said. She didn't realize she had said it in Portuguese until Hiro echoed in

Japanese, "Soko!"

She turned the wheel, feathered the throttle to keep from launching them, and felt the hull's complaint through her knees.

The shape resolved into a dinghy—a cheap lab tender. It rocked too hard, showed too much of its underside, an animal on its back. Two figures in it: one hunched at the oars, spiky hair plastered black, the other a long shape in the stern, still and wrong.

Sofia's stomach folded on itself and kept folding.

Waves shouldered in pairs now, mean little brothers to the giants of the night before. Wind found a new register and whistled. Lightning spidered a polite distance away and showed her, for a flash, the dinghy tipping, catching itself, tipping again. Thunder followed like a late answer.

"Hold on," she told Hiro. It came out calm.

She poured speed into the gap. The bow smacked a trough, climbed a face, smacked another. Spray needled; her bandaged hand burned. The storm ahead hunched its massive back and started to run.

She couldn't see faces yet. Could see movement—frantic, then not. Could see a pair of oars dip, catch, slip. Could see a long, bound outline slide two inches toward water, then stop, then slide again.

Time shortened. The world sharpened. She leaned the boat into the hurtling geometry of waves and counted without realizing she'd started. Ten swells to close half the distance. Eight. Five. The dinghy yawed in a gust and showed her, for a heart's beat, the profile of the rower's face.

Blue hair plastered flat. Mascara like warpaint. Eyes wild as a trapped animal's.

"Emi," Hiro whispered, as if the name itself could be a rope.

Lightning scored the horizon. Thunder answered, closer. The storm opened its hand and let the first fat drops fall between them and the dinghy—cold coins hammered down by wind.

Sofia pushed the throttle forward one more notch. The little boat ahead rocked so hard it showed its ribs. The longer shape in the stern slid another inch toward the rim.

She still couldn't quite make out who that was. She didn't need to. Time had become the only meaningful noun. The storm was a giant coming at a run.

Sofia set her jaw. "Hold together," she told the boat.

"Hold together," she told herself.

And she went faster.

CHAPTER 26

The storm found them.

Wind shouldered the boat sideways and the sea rose into black geometry—steep faces, quick troughs, a treacherous shuffle. Sofia rode the throttle like a violin bow, easing then feeding power, keeping the bow half a breath off disaster. The dinghy pitched ahead, a toy in a hungry dog's mouth.

"Emi!" Hiro shouted, cupping his hands. The wind took his voice and chewed it.

Sofia angled across the swell and closed the last cruel meters. Lightning tore a white gash in the sky and for an instant she saw everything too clearly: Emi's spiky blue hair plastered to her skull, mascara like war paint; Mila in the stern, bound, breathing—breathing—color gone, lips blueing; a squat river anchor in the footwell, chain leading to Mila's ankles; a second length of chain looped twice around Emi's waist, the loose end clasped with a cheap D-shackle.

"Emi!" Sofia shouted. "Stop. Listen to me."

Emi looked at her, and the look was a wound—defiant, desperate, gathering itself for a leap. She wrapped her arms tighter around Mila as if to fuse them by force.

Sofia's mind slid into the old, clean rails: buy time; lower your voice when they raise theirs; name the feeling before you name the ask; give them a smaller bridge to cross.

"You're scared," she called, steady. "And you're right to be. Love can turn a person inside out. It makes us all stupid and holy and dangerous. I know that. I know that."

Emi squeezed her eyes shut like a child refusing medicine. "Go away!"

"We can talk on a dock," Sofia said, and put a hand up, palm showing, no threat. "Where you can hear yourself. You don't have to do this out here."

Wind slapped spray across both boats. The dinghy slewed broadside and slammed against Sofia's hull—wood on fiberglass, an awful, cracking kiss. The little craft bounced back, took on a gulp of water, and settled lower. Mila flinched as the chain jerked; a small sound escaped her, more exhale than voice.

"Mila," Sofia called, uselessly, because the name was partly for herself. She felt a wild, dizzy elation bloom and break. Alive. They had been wrong and also right—wrong about the death, right about the danger. Relief and horror arrived married.

"Emi," Hiro tried again, voice breaking. "Please. Please."

Emi ignored him, dug in an oar, hauled the dinghy closer to the open mouth of the waves like she could row into oblivion faster. She looked at Sofia again, chin trembling. "We were meant," she said, the words hitching. "Nobody understands."

Sofia felt the chain of questions she could ask—the drill, the ladder, the trap. But the storm did not have rungs. It had moments. She would have to span the gap in one throw.

"You're not wrong about the pain," Sofia said, and felt something raw unbutton in her chest. She didn't soften her voice; she let it carry. "Losing someone splits you. It makes the world tilt and never go back. I—" She stopped and swallowed hard, because saying his name was like stepping barefoot on glass. "Julian is gone." The words came out flat and present-tense and true. "He fell. I watched him fall. And the sea kept him."

Mila jerked, a tiny panic, at her brother's name. Emi stared.

"I found warmth," Sofia said, and the storm blurred. "For the first time in—God, I don't know—years. Maybe ever. And the sea took it. There wasn't anything noble about it. There wasn't a lesson. It was just… gone." She realized she was crying only because the salt on her lips tasted wrong.

Emi's face crumpled, the fury in it collapsing under something softer and more lethal. Tears cut new tracks through the black. "I love her," she said, almost conversationally, like reporting a weather observation. "I love her so much it hurts my bones."

"I believe you," Sofia said, and she did. "So do the thing love wants that obsession can't—keep her breathing." She edged the wheel, lining the boats. "You can still choose that."

The dinghy lurched again; the next wave taller, meaner. When it slammed, the starboard gunwale cracked with a splintering pop and sank an inch. Water sheeted in. The anchor chain clinked and tightened at Mila's ankles.

"We're out of time," Sofia said to no one and everyone.

She brought the boat alongside with a movement that was more prayer than seamanship. The hulls kissed and bit. "Hold us!" she shouted. Hiro was already there, slamming a boat hook across, wedging wood into wood, bracing with his whole slight body. The two craft ground against each other in the surge. Another inch of dinghy disappeared.

Sofia didn't think. She moved.

She jumped.

Her boots hit flooded wood; cold climbed her legs like hands. The dinghy heeled sickeningly and then settled with a slurp. Emi snarled, animal and human at once, and lunged. They collided in the cramped space —elbows, breath, a tangle of wet limbs. Emi clawed for the chain; Sofia shoved her back, felt nails rake her injured hand, saw white pain explode and float.

"Leave us alone!" Emi screamed. "You don't get it—you break everything—he broke everything—"

Sofia ducked a flailing elbow, hooked her arm around Emi's shoulders, turned the movement into an awkward embrace that stole leverage. "I get it enough to tell you this will only make the pain permanent."

"Love is supposed to hurt," Emi spat, sobbing.

"Not like this."

Lightning stitched the sky so close the hair on Sofia's neck rose. The thunder that followed was a punch to the chest. The dinghy heaved; water sloshed to Sofia's knees. Mila's eyes fluttered. She was there and not there, shivering in little, obedient tremors.

The chain at her ankles was looped through with a rusted D-shackle, the thumb screw crusted with salt. Sofia dropped to her knees, hands already on the hardware, fingers fumbling. Her bandaged palm screamed when she tried to turn the screw. It wouldn't budge. She set her teeth and tried again. It moved a fraction, then froze.

"Give it to me," Emi said, sudden and terribly calm, reaching for the shackle like a mother for a buckle. "I can do it. And then we go."

Sofia batted her hand away. "No."

She braced the shackle against the dinghy's seat and used her good hand and the heel of her bad one to torque. The head gave, begrudgingly, then another half turn. A gust hit; the boats slammed again; Hiro grunted, straining to keep them together. "Sofia!"

"Almost," she breathed, and was not sure if it was promise or lie.

The screw finally spun free. She yanked the pin, knocked it against her knuckles, slid the chain out and kicked the squat anchor under the seat, wedging it with her boot. "Mila," she said, trying to find the woman's face. "Stay with me."

Emi had looped the other chain twice around her own waist and clipped it with the same cheap shackle. Her hands shook as she tightened it, lips moving—prayer, apology, both. She looked at Mila, and the look emptied her. Then she looked at Sofia.

For a heartbeat Sofia saw her as she might have been—bright, ferocious, wired for wonder—standing on a dock with a clipboard and a grin, not here with a chain and a death wish. The storm roared. The boats groaned. There was no eloquence left that could span this gap.

"Emi," Hiro said, voice breaking on the second syllable. "Please."

Emi's eyes flicked to him, softening for a fraction. She opened her mouth and closed it. Then she stepped backward onto the gunwale, the chain clinking. She did not say anything else. She simply leaned and let the ocean take her.

"No!" Hiro shouted, the sound torn away.

Sofia lunged, fingers snagging wet air and nothing else. The chain paid out in a bright, brief stream and then jerked and went quiet as the anchor under the seat pinned it. Bubbles boiled up and burst. The water closed its smooth hand over where a girl had been.

The dinghy sagged. Water poured in,

heavy now, indifferent. Mila made a small noise—a protest or a dream.

"Go!" Sofia yelled at herself and the world. She slid her arms under Mila's shoulders, felt the dead weight of exhaustion and cold and fear. "Hiro—now!"

He was already scrambling across the gap, feet wide, boat hook braced like a bridge. He grabbed Mila's forearms as Sofia lifted. The dinghy tried to roll; Sofia threw her weight the other way, the wounded hand screaming. "One —two—" she counted in Portuguese because that was the language in which hard things sometimes obeyed. "—three."

They heaved. Mila's body came up out of the dinghy and caught on the gunwale and then over, dragging Hiro forward onto his knees on the bigger boat's deck. Mila's ankle was bruised from where the chain had been removed in the last moment. But other than that, Sofia didn't see any visible injuries. Hiro gathered her against him, whispering her name, over and over, like a rope of sound.

The dinghy, relieved of its last, noble task, sighed and rolled. Water took it. The little anchor clunked once against wood and disappeared into green.

Sofia grabbed the rail and hauled herself across, legs heavy, breath burning. She tumbled into the cockpit as a wave broke over the bow and ran past, a sheet of cold slap. She scrambled to the helm, slammed the throttle forward, and spun the wheel to put their bow into the worst of it.

Mila coughed—small and awful—and turned her face blindly into Hiro's shoulder. He wrapped himself around her like a shield. He pressed his mouth to her wet hair, eyes closed, tears indistinguishable from the rain. "I've got you," he said, voice wrecked. "I've got you."

Lightning scratched the dark; thunder thumped their bones. The storm leaned harder, but the borrowed boat had more to give than the dinghy had—weight and keel and a will built into its planks. Sofia felt it square its shoulders and climb.

She set a course that was mostly a hope and partly a bearing toward the dull glow that meant town. The engine labored and then found its note. The bow rose and fell and rose. The wharf lights blinked like tired saints.

Hiro held Mila, rocking with the boat, murmuring nothing words that meant everything. Mila's fingers found the fabric of his jacket and pinched, a small, stubborn anchor to the living.

Sofia kept her eyes on the dark ahead where the channel should be. Tears slicked her cheeks and stuck in the wind like sea-spray, and she let them. She did not have hands free to wipe them away.

Julian was not on this boat. The sea had not returned him. The space where he should have been stood at her shoulder like a man made of air. She drove into the weather with him there, the ache a steadying weight.

Behind them, the storm reached with long fingers and found only wake. Ahead, the breakwater opened its mouth. The boat slid through.

Mila was alive. Sofia repeated it the way a person repeats the names of saints.

Alive. Alive. Alive.

CHAPTER 27

The Alfama light was kind to the tired. It slipped down the steep street in a honeyed spill, catching on tram wires and azulejo tiles, softening everything it touched. Sofia and Nuno shared a small iron table outside the bookshop, two cups steaming between them. He read with a finger marking his place, glasses low on his nose, cardigan sleeves rolled just so; she cupped her tea and let the heat do the talking her mouth couldn't.

Silence sat with them like an old friend. The shop's sign creaked once. Somewhere behind them a kettle clicked and went quiet. She had missed this—the comfort of someone who required nothing, the way being near Nuno felt like standing in the lee of a sturdy wall on a windy day. And yet the center of her chest was hollowed out, a wound with edges too clean to make sense. She had opened the door she kept bolted. The sea had reached in and taken what it wanted.

After a long while she said, "Your lemon balm is stronger this year."

Nuno lifted his eyes, nodded. "The plant likes neglect," he said. "I am an excellent neglecter." The ghost of a smile, then quiet again. He turned a page and asked, mildly, "And you? Are you sleeping like a cat in sun—or like a soldier in a trench?"

"Both," she said. They drifted back into the hush.

Across the street, a delivery boy chased a runaway pastelaria box, laughing as the white twine unraveled behind him like a comet tail. Two little girls hopped a chalked-out hopscotch while their grandmother scolded the sky for threatening rain. Tram 28 dinged its brass bell and slid by, passengers pressed to the windows as if curiosity itself were a seat. A dog shook off a bath in the doorway of a bar, spraying arc-light onto a row of beer crates; the bartender clapped and whooped at the mess.

Sofia watched it and felt none of it land. Cheer was something happening on the far side of glass. She set her cup down and stood. "I'm going inside."

Nuno didn't ask why. He closed his book on a finger, rose with the careful grace of a tall man who knows old joints have opinions, and followed.

The bell over the door chimed. Inside, the

air smelled of paper and dust and lemon balm tea, with a thread of ink that clung to Nuno the way sea-salt clings to nets. Shelves marched in tidy ranks, spines labeled in his neat hand: atlases, poetry, maritime law, a whole wall of crime novels with little paper flags marking favorite chapters. A ladder waited at the end of a rail. On the counter sat a dish of pressed leaves—bookmarks in another life—and a ceramic cup full of pencils, all sharpened to the same degree. He kept a miniature broom by the register and used it.

Behind the shop proper, the bachelor pad unfolded in quiet, domestic grammar: a narrow kitchen with a gas ring and a jar of questionable kombucha scowling gently in a corner; a table with three placemats though he rarely hosted three; a tweed coat hung by the door with postcards tucked into its inner pocket; a cot made with military precision and a wool throw folded at its foot; rows of boxes labeled in his careful block letters—CASE FILES (OLD), MAPS (COASTAL), LETTERS (UNSENT). Everything was in its place. It always had been.

They moved through the little space without talking, practiced as tide and shore. When she paused to look at nothing in particular, he set his hand at the small of her back, steadying without steering. She leaned back, and then turned and put her arms around him. It was the hundredth time that day. He made the same soft sound he always made—surprise, then acceptance—and folded her in.

"You can stay as long as you want," he said into her hair.

She didn't move.

He eased back enough to see her face and said it again, slower, letting each word find its chair. "I want you to stay as long as you want. You are welcome as long as you need. You are always welcome." His blue-gray eyes softened. "You are family, menina."

The word undid a knot she hadn't realized she'd been cinching tighter to keep the world from falling out. Tears came quick and hot. He held her until the worst of the shaking passed, one hand still steady at her back, the other smoothing a line no one else would have noticed was ruffled.

"I don't care about Valezzi," she said into his sweater, the consonants catching. "Not today. Not the yacht. Not the cases. I'm… empty." She took a breath that shuddered at the edges. "I'm glad Mila is alive. I am. But I—" The rest fell into the hollow space and stayed there. She didn't have words for the way the world had tilted since the cliff.

Nuno didn't try to fill the silence with answers that would be lies. "We will put the kettle on," he said finally. "We will make the bed. We will listen to the rain criticize Lisbon. And when you want to talk about anything—your mother's songs, or the pencil you carry, or nothing at all—we will talk." He tucked a stray hair behind her ear with the gentleness he reserved for first editions. "Until then we will breathe."

She nodded against him. The emptiness didn't shrink, but it stopped feeling like falling. The shop settled around them—the murmur of the street through old glass, the tick of the clock above the atlas case, the faint fizz of a kombucha jar.

Sofia let her eyes close. In the darkness behind her lids, waves rose and fell and, eventually, calmed. She did not whisper her calming words. She didn't need to. For the first time since the cliff, the quiet felt like a thing she could live in. Nuno's hand stayed at her back. The city breathed. Somewhere beyond, a tram dinged again, polite as a friend at the door.

She missed Julian with a fierceness that was almost clean in its simplicity. She would miss him for a long time. She knew this. For now, she let herself be held, and let Lisbon be a place that held things without demanding they be fixed.

"Stay," Nuno said once more, as if naming it could keep it true.

She stayed.

EPILOGUE:

He felt the prison before he saw it.

Vibration, not sound: a low shiver through concrete and rebar, the slow pulse of generators in the earth. The bulb on the landing jittered in its cage and threw a pale, tired circle that followed him down. He moved without hurry, big shoulders grazing damp walls, the AK-47 resting easy in the crook of his arm like a sleeping dog. Tattoos coiled from wrist to elbow—dragons and rope and a compass that pointed nowhere. His skull was slick and scarred where ears should have been. Scar tissue knotted his lips into an old, permanent hush. There was no tongue behind them. There were no words.

He counted the steps by feel. Twenty-one to the first grate. Twenty-one to the second. The scent of rust and bleach and men crowded the corridor like a weather front. Through the first door's slot, a shadow uncoiled from a wall chain, lips forming a plea he would never hear. Through the second, two shapes, knees up, foreheads pressed to flaking paint, the rhythm of their breathing a small tremor underfoot. He did not stop. He was the kind of man who learned a place with his body. He knew which hinges complained against the bar, which padlock had a tooth that stuck, which section of the corridor had been poured thinner than the rest.

At the end, the new door waited. It had no number, only a slash of chalk that had already started to run in the damp. The note on his belt —folded once, then again—had said simply: Delivered by the Ghost. Hold. The words were for other men. He needed only the weight of them.

The Ghost made men shake. Even men like him. Even without ears.

He peered through the slot. The cell was a rectangle of gray and iron. Chains bit from a ring in the wall— On the far side, a man sat with his back to the concrete, wrists bound above his head, head tipped like a boxer catching breath between rounds. When the guard's shadow cut the slot, the man looked up.

Blue eyes.

They were swollen at the corners and raw as sea-salt, but blue still, startling in the half-dark. The guard cataloged the details without judgment, the way he had been taught:

cheekbone split, lower lip cut, cheap bandage around the ribs pulled too tight by someone in a hurry. A cuff mark on the left wrist, newer than the one on the right. Nails clean.

The man with blue eyes took him in: the bulk at the door, the rifle, the ruin where ears should have been, the mouth that could not shape Yes or No. Something like calculation crossed the prisoner's face. It faded. He stared at the guard openly. Not challenge. Not surrender. A simple, stubborn refusal to be less than a person.

The guard held his gaze as long as it was held. He had learned this, too—some men needed to be seen to make it through the next minute. It cost him nothing. He had nothing to spend.

He slid a tin cup through the slot and waited. The man shifted, tested the chain without noise, and managed a swallow. When the cup came back, the guard took it, set it on the cart, and did not look at the water left inside. He palmed the key that was not a key—metal bump with a notch filed just so—and checked the shackles with the same sure indifference with which he checked every shackle, every night. He pressed the links, tested the anchor bolt. Solid. The Ghost's work was always solid.

He stepped back. The blue-eyed man closed his eyes and opened them. He was not praying. He was counting, maybe. He was remembering a name he could not afford to say out loud in that room..

Down here, names fell away. Down here, hunger and time did their work. Down here, a life was as long as she decided.

For the man in the last cell, she had decided not long.

Continues in Book 8: The Siren's Shadow

The master thief came to steal a legendary sapphire and slipped beneath a Paris limousine—only to find a dead heiress where the jewel should have been.

Read by clicking this link: https://www.amazon.com/gp/product/B0FST2NPPH

(The Siren's Shadow by Georgia Wagner can be found on Amazon.com)

Sneak Preview of The Siren's Shadow below!

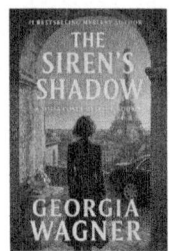

PROLOGUE — PLACE VENDÔME, PARIS

Place Vendôme looked asleep. It was not.

He arrived on foot, as if he belonged to the hour—a slim, dapper silhouette in a rain-dark coat, cufflinks dulled with carbon tape. He had already memorized the guards' routes: a three-minute loop along the arcade, a two-minute pause under the portico, radios chirring on the half minute. He watched them once, twice, not because he needed to, but because he liked the certainty of being right. Then he moved.

A wrought-iron delivery gate barred the service passage. He slipped a thin wedge into the latch, eased pressure, felt the deadbolt float, and threaded himself sideways through the opening. Cameras blinked from the cornice—little black commas on cream stone. He kept to the blind seams he had mapped earlier, gliding from column to column as if the air itself had edges.

The alley beyond smelled of beeswax and wet stone. He stopped at the curb where the maison's armored sedan dozed beneath a sheen of drizzle. A small magnet clicked under the bumper; his gloved hands found purchase on chassis and cross-member, and he slid beneath the car, body flat, breath measured. The engine turned over; the vehicle rolled. He went with it, a barnacle in a bespoke suit.

The sedan nosed into a private courtyard. He timed the crawl with his watch haptics —two long pulses, one short—counting the exact stretch between the rear wheels and a low, iron-bound cellar door. When the driver braked to buzz the inner gate, the car yawed, the rear tire dipped into the drainage rut, and the undercarriage rose a whisper.

He released.

Gravity gave him to the cobbles. He rolled onto a rubberized mat he'd laid during an earlier delivery, sound swallowed. Twenty-five seconds—that was the hole in the pattern, the sliver he had cut from a night of watching men bored with safety.

He was already at the door.

A practiced pressure on the cylinder with

a featherlight tension wrench; a Bogotá rake teased the pins; the lock spoke to him in tiny clicks, tumblers falling like rain.

Fifteen seconds. Twelve.

He set the wrench, went to single-pin picking. Seven. The bolt slid.

He slipped inside, closed the door behind him, and let a grin touch his mouth. So far, it felt like art—precision and breath, a private dance.

The cellar was a spine of vaulted brick and galvanized conduit, the air cool and machine-clean. He moved in a half-crouch, lamp off, counting the junctions by his soles. Where the passage widened he paused, misted the air. A faint lattice of infrared woke into existence—red threads trembling in the draft, a cat's cradle between wall sensors. He took a mirror from his pocket, the size of a postage stamp on a wire, tilted beams to kiss the opposite nodes while he slid through the diamond-shaped void between them. At the far wall he exhaled, replaced the mirror, and felt a quick, delighted heat in his chest. The Fox would have approved.

A service stair rose to the ground floor. More guards above. He pressed an ear—not to listen (there was nothing to hear but his own blood)—but to feel the faintest tremor of footsteps through ancient stone. Left. Right. Away.

He took the stairs like a rumor, the last three at speed, then sprang, catching the underside of the banister and moving hand-over-hand along its smooth belly to avoid the pressure sensors in the treads.

The balustrade spit him onto the mezzanine. Beyond the glass doors, the salon slept: vitrines like black monoliths, velvet walls absorbing the light. He tried the handle. Locked. The bypass would burn time he did not own.

So he went loud.

His elbow met tempered glass. It chimed and flowered into a thousand glittering scales. Alarms woke everywhere at once, shrill and certain. He glanced at his watch: fifty seconds before internal shutters fell like metal eyelids. Fifty seconds before the square's private response team boiled through the front.

He ran.

He knew precisely where *La Sirène de Minuit* should have been kept until morning—behind the mirrored panel, through the smart-lock at the archive corridor, inside the vault room with humidity as steady as prayer. The passcode danced under his fingers; he killed the door contact with a magnet the size of a seed and slid through the seam.

The vault room was wrong.

He went very still. No sapphire. No vitrine. On the floor, a dark glisten that had already begun to tack at the edges.

There, death.

A body—face turned away, one hand flung open in a frozen reach toward nothing. Next to it lay a weapon that didn't belong to the century: a medieval flanged mace, French work, steel petals dark with age and something newer. The kind of thing knights would have swung in a press of men, reproduced these days for museums and the very rich.

His mouth moved and made a word because there was no better one.

"Merde."

No stone. No time. Forty seconds.

He stared at the corpse. The victim's evening suit had splayed under the fall, collar askew. Around that throat—because Paris is vain even in catastrophe—glittered a rivière of diamonds, an old cut, almost certainly insured and absolutely not bolted to the floor.

He didn't want to leave with nothing.

His knife was a whisper. The clasp

surrendered. He palmed the necklace, slid it into an inside pocket where the lining had been cut for a reason, then lifted his head at the change in the air—the whump of shutters beginning to descend somewhere deep, the building taking a breath before it closed its throat.

Thirty seconds.

He turned and ran the way he had not come. Through a staff pantry, across a polished corridor that showed his blurred reflection, into a side office with a window latched against a square of exactly Paris blue-black. He raised his elbow again, shielded his face with his forearm, and the glass cried and broke.

Wind shoved its hand inside. He climbed onto the sill, swung out, and found the cold mouth of a copper drainage pipe with his fingers. The pipe sang under his weight; he slid, boots hissing with friction and rain. Halfway down he kicked out, landed on a stone ledge that pretended to be decor, and dropped the last two meters into an alley where the air tasted like oil and old champagne.

The alarms were full-throated now, echoing between walls, catching on the bronze column and flinging themselves back. He ran bent at the waist, felt the square at his left shoulder like a watchful eye, cut behind a stack of catering crates, and reached the narrow gap where the scooter waited.

"Go," he snapped, the single syllable bitten in half.

The rider didn't ask. The machine leapt, tires spitting on slick cobbles. Place Vendôme slid behind them, stately and furious, all those stone faces pretending not to stare.

He gave the square one last look as they shot into Rue de la Paix—at the lighted windows, the men already spilling like ants from the arcades, the idea of a sapphire glowing someplace it should not. Anger climbed his ribs like a ladder. He had charted every guard's pause and every camera's blink; he had timed his breath to the square. He had executed something close to perfect.

And inside the dragon's hoard, the dragon had already been and gone.

He tightened his jaw, felt the hard, cool weight of diamonds against his ribs, and let fury do what it always did for him—sharpen the next cut.

CHAPTER 1
— LISBON

Grief had learned her address; it slipped its mail through the slot each morning with the Tagus light.

Sofia stood in the doorway of the Alfama bookshop and watched Lisbon come awake—laundry strung between balconies, swallows scribbling the air, the blue tiles across the lane catching sunlight like water. Behind her, the little bell over the door pinged as Nuno Silva closed it against the breeze, the scent of lemon balm tea and old paper holding steady in the hush.

He looked as he always had and a touch better: tall and spare, salt-and-pepper hair tied back in a low knot, a neatly trimmed beard on a long, sun-lined face. The blue-gray of his eyes still carried that far-off cast of a man who replayed conversations from twenty years ago. He wore his familiar cardigan over an old dress shirt, a tweed coat slung on the chair back—inside pockets fat with folded papers he would deny existed if anyone asked. Four months retired from Interpol, and trouble still sat at his elbow like a cat that knew the sound of its dish.

On the counter, a laptop glowed with the sort of interface no civilian ought to have. He was whistling—off-key, unrepentant—as he scrolled.

Sofia leaned a shoulder to the doorjamb. "If you whistle any happier, the tiles will start clapping."

Nuno clicked a window closed with an innocence better suited to altar boys. "I am happy," he said in Portuguese, the vowels round and soft. "You are here."

She stepped beside him, the yellow pencil tucked in her messy bun a small, loyal weight. In the laptop's reflection she saw word-blocks and call signs and a cartoon octopus holding a knife. "Don't," she said.

"What?" He rearranged his face into wonder. "I am retired. I am reading about fish."

"You are 'reading' Yakuza chatter out of Yokohama," she said. "Interpol eyes-on. Changing the font doesn't make it poetry."

He grimaced, then lifted a porcelain cup and took a penitent sip of kombucha. He drank less of the stuff since she'd moved in five weeks ago, but the brew still lined the high shelf like amber saints. "They talk too much," he said. "It is a public service to be bored by them."

"I don't want to hear any of it." She tucked a stray strand behind her ear; the scar along her left eyebrow tugged the skin, an old weather vane. She was tired in a way that had nothing to do with sleep.

The nights came in shards: the cliff, the spray, Julian's blue eyes bright and then gone.

Nuno turned the laptop fully shut, neat as a clasp. He studied her with the care he used to save for bombs and children. "You slept?"

She could have lied; he would have known. "Some," she said, and the word broke in two.

In his shop she had found the only quiet that did not feel like a lie. He was different with her upstairs—lighter, somehow. She had never known him to whistle. It had made her smile when she heard it over the kettle at dawn, the sound wobbling slightly as if unsure of its welcome.

He reached behind him, produced a paperback wrapped in clear film. Brushstroked characters marched down the cover. "For you."

"I don't read Chinese," she said. "Yet."

"You learn fast." The corner of his mouth

eased upward. "By the end of a coffee, eight languages fall out of your sleeve. This one is a detective. The sentences are short. They will like you."

She slid the book into her satchel beside a battered leather notebook, the passports she wasn't using, the old Seiko watch that had survived three continents and one rude swim. Layered jacket, neutral scarf, scuffed ankle boots—her armor of ordinary. "Later," she said. "I have a meeting."

Nuno's attention sharpened. "With whom?"

"Someone who can give me what I need." A breath. "A face that isn't mine. A name that won't catch in the wrong net."

His brow creased, that thin vertical line she had known since the day he'd taught her how to ask a question that didn't sound like one. "Isabella Calderón," he said, almost sighing the name.

Sofia looked up through her lashes. "What did I tell you about reading my text messages?"

"I haven't been," he said, hands open.

"You haven't been looking at my phone," she corrected, "but that doesn't mean you're not intercepting my communications. That's not what friends do."

He lifted the kombucha again and let it hover, as if the glass might hide him. "I am worried about you, *miúda*. That is what friends do."

He didn't quite meet her eyes. He didn't have to. The conversation stood between them like an extra chair. Valezzi had drawn blood and would want more; the woman collected debts the way other people collected wine. Nuno believed his bookshop was a kind of sanctuary, paper walls warding off a storm. Sofia didn't trust walls; she trusted flight.

"She killed him," she said, because some truths insisted on air. "She won't stop with me alive."

"You are safe here," he answered too quickly.

"You think you are safe here," she said, soft rather than sharp. "That isn't the same."

They had gone around this circle three times in the last week and twice at two a.m., both of them too stubborn to get off. Today she meant to cut through. There were two people on earth she trusted to dismantle a face and put it back better—Isabella Calderón and her twin brother. The twins had moved their meeting twice. A week had slipped. Worry simmered where patience should be.

She stepped close and put her arms

around him. He stiffened, surprised, then softened like bread under heat. She kissed his cheek. He blushed like a young man and muttered, very low, "*A Bela e o Monstro*."

That made her laugh, a small sound that didn't entirely hurt. "That makes you the beauty."

"Do not blaspheme." He recovered enough to pat her shoulder—awkward, precise—and then nodded toward the door. "Where are you going?"

"Chiado," she said. "Café A Brasileira. Ten o'clock. If the bronze poet tries to flirt, I'll send him home."

Nuno's mouth twitched. "Pessoa had terrible manners."

"He's a statue," she said. "He can get away with it."

"Will you be back for dinner?" he asked, too casual to be casual.

"Yes."

"Should we expect guests?" His eyes were almost innocent.

She shook her head. He winked. "There are many handsome men in Lisbon."

"Oh, *por favor*," she said, rolling her eyes. He had tried to set her up with the mailman two weeks ago—a gentle man with a dimple and exactly zero chance. It was not subtle and it was not unwelcome in the way a hot-water bottle is not unwelcome: homely, kind, an attempt at comfort in a cold bed.

She clipped the satchel strap across her chest. He watched her, his worry tucked inside his ribs like contraband. "You will come back," he said.

"I will." She meant it. She wanted it to be true.

Outside, Alfama's lanes curled downhill like spilled ribbon. She cut across the little square, down the steps where the tile saints kept their vigil, and into the brightness of Rua da Madalena. Lisbon did what it always did —offered up its color as consolation. Purple jacaranda dropped confetti on scooters. A woman hung white sheets that clapped like slow applause. A tram squealed past, yellow and stubborn as a canary that wouldn't leave its perch. The air tasted of coffee and river and salt.

She passed a café where men in flat caps argued about football and metaphysics with equal vigor. The waiter called her *menina* and offered a pastel; she smiled and shook her head.

At the top of the Baixa she paused and

looked down the long spill of Rua Augusta to the arch and the square beyond, the river broad and blunt with light. Sometimes beauty annoyed her with its timing.

Her phone thrummed in her pocket. She pulled it out without breaking stride. *Unknown* at the top; a text that wasn't careful enough to be truly anonymous.

Change of plan. Convento do Carmo. Cloister, north side. 10:15. Sorry—last minute issue.

Sofia slowed. The Carmo ruins were five minutes from A Brasileira, tourist-thick and easy to vanish in. But Izzy wasn't flighty; that was Luca's specialty. The sister—the disguise artist, the one who could make cheekbones into weapons. Last-minute wasn't her style.

Sofia typed back: *OK. See you there.* Then added nothing else. She slid the phone away and kept moving, faster now, threading the narrow Rua Garrett with the rest of the morning crowd. In her head, the old ritual rose unbidden and did its work.

"*Bezopasnost,*" she murmured. "*Seguridad. Ān quán.*"

Her pulse steadied. She adjusted the strap on her satchel. The arch of the sky above Chiado opened wide and clean; somewhere a guitarist teased *fado* out of a cheap amp and made it sound like memory. She didn't want to think, but her mind did what it always did—built patterns, tested seams.

Why the move? Why there?

She reached Largo do Carmo as the bells of the police museum chimed the quarter. Tour groups drifted like slow fish through the square. The ruins rose at the edge—nave roof gone since 1755, ribs of stone open to sky. The cloister lay beyond, cooler, quieter, a place where voices turned reverent without meaning to. She scanned faces out of habit, caught languages in snippets—French, German, a Midwestern couple grading pastries like exam papers.

Her phone hummed once more in her pocket, a phantom buzz she felt even after it stilled. She picked up her pace, eyes narrowed, the pencil in her hair a little weight reminding her who she was even when she borrowed other names.

She was Sofia Costa. She found people. She found truth. And if Izzy Calderón was changing the script, there was a reason.

Continues in Book 8: The Siren's Shadow

The master thief came to steal a legendary sapphire and slipped beneath a Paris limousine— only to find a dead heiress where the jewel should have been.

Read by clicking this link: https://www.amazon.com/gp/product/B0FST2NPPH

(The Siren's Shadow by Georgia Wagner can be found on Amazon.com)

WANT A BOOK DEDICATED TO YOU AND A FREE MYSTERY STORY?

Join Georgia Wagner's Mailing List and you could be the monthly pick for a dedication.

-Help name characters & vote on settings (Egyptian desert or Swiss Alps? You decide).

-Get free bonus stories and behind-the-scenes updates. (*Download The Board Between Them, an Artemis Blythe and Wren Cade Short Story*)

-List members are thanked in Acknowledgments.

Join now → https://dl.bookfunnel.com/t00lirmst4

TEMPEST OF SECRETS: SOFIA COSTA MYSTERIES BOOK...

Printed in Dunstable, United Kingdom